werewolf legends and werewolf facts, according to grandma

On the power of the moon: "For three days, the moon is full enough to boil the blood and make a man turn wolf. The second day the curse is at its strongest, and the higher the moon is in the sky, the more deadly the wolf."

On werewolf appetites: "In human form, they can eat anything humans eat, although they're partial to meat. In wolf form, they're driven to eat their weight in meat each night, and it must be the meat of a fresh kill."

On the mind of the werewolf: "The mind of a human infected with the werewolf curse doesn't always start off being evil, but the way I see it, a person turns evil real quick."

On werewolf redemption: "Ain't no such thing. No antidote, no remedy, no turning back. Only way to save a werewolf's soul is to end its misery, and hope the good Lord truly does have infinite mercy."

On the chances of surviving a werewolf: "We all have to die someday. Let's hope we die as humans."

OTHER SPEAK BOOKS

NEAL SHUSTERMAN

darkfusion ▲ BOOK 2

Red Rider's Hood

speak

An Imprint of Penguin Group (USA) Inc.

SPEAK

Published by the Penguin Group
Penguin Group (USA) Inc.,
345 Hudson Street, New York, New York 10014, U.S.A.
Penguin Group (Canada), 90 Eglinton Avenue East, Suite 700, Toronto,
Ontario, Canada M4P 2Y3 (a division of Pearson Penguin Canada Inc.)
Penguin Books Ltd, 80 Strand, London WC2R 0RL, England
Penguin Ireland, 25 St Stephen's Green, Dublin 2, Ireland
(a division of Penguin Books Ltd)
Penguin Group (Australia), 250 Camberwell Road, Camberwell, Victoria 3124, Australia
(a division of Pearson Australia Group Pty Ltd)
Penguin Books India Pvt Ltd, 11 Community Centre, Panchsheel Park, New Delhi - 110 017, India
Penguin Group (NZ), Cnr Airborne and Rosedale Roads, Albany, Auckland 1310,
New Zealand (a division of Pearson New Zealand Ltd)
Penguin Books (South Africa) (Pty) Ltd, 24 Sturdee Avenue,
Rosebank, Johannesburg 2196, South Africa

Registered Offices: Penguin Books Ltd, 80 Strand, London WC2R 0RL, England

First published in the United States of America by Dutton Children's Books,
a division of Penguin Young Readers Group, 2005
Published by Speak, an imprint of Penguin Group (USA) Inc., 2006

1 3 5 7 9 10 8 6 4 2

Copyright © Neal Shusterman, 2005

CIP Data is available.

Speak ISBN 0-14-240678-3

Designed by Jason Henry

Printed in the United States of America

For Steve Layne

1
RED AS FRESH BLOOD

It's a jungle out there. Buildings grow all around you out of the cracking pavement, blocking out the daylight, making you forget the sun's there at all. Those buildings can't block out the moonlight, though. Nothing can block that out. Trust me, I know.

I can't tell you my name, because then you'd be in danger, too. I got enemies, see, and the only reason I'm alive right now is because my Mustang convertible—red as fresh blood, and as powerful as they come—is faster than anyone, or any *thing,* can run. You can call me Red. Red Rider. It's what they called me back when I had my old Radio Flyer wagon as a kid, and it's what they call me now.

As for the Mustang, I found it in a junkyard when I was thir-teen, and spent three years nursing it back to health. Call it a hobby. By the time I turned sixteen—which was on the last day of the school year—it was ready for me to drive. Little did I know what I'd be driving myself into that hot and horrible summer.

See, when you ride out into these streets, you never know what you're in for. Good or bad; thrilling or dangerous. Sometimes it's a little bit of both. It's not that my neighborhood's an awful place, but it's crowded. We got every culture here: Hispanic, African-American, white, Vietnamese, Armenian—you name it. We're this big melting pot, but someone turned up the heat too high, and the stew started to burn. Gangs, crime, fights, and fear are now a regular part of our local stew.

It all started the day I had to deliver some "bread" to my grandma. That's what she calls money, because she's still stuck in the sixties, when money was "bread," cops were "fuzz," and everything else was "groovy." Don't even bother telling her it's a whole other millennium. Going to her house, you'd think the sixties never ended. There are love beads hanging in doorways, Jimi Hendrix playing on an old record player, and a big old Afro on her head. It really ticks people off in movie theaters, because when Grandma sits down, there's nothing but hair for the people behind her. And the funny thing is, she's not even black. She married a black man, though, and their daughter married a Korean, and that's how they got me. I guess I'll marry a Puerto Rican girl or something, and fill out that gene pool swimming inside me.

Anyway, Grandma didn't believe in banks, because her father lost all his money in the crash of 1929. Grandma made our whole family swear by cast-iron safes hidden behind paintings. For some reason, our house became the main branch.

"You take this bag to your grandma first thing in the morning, and don't stop for anything on the way," my mom instructed me. She knew how much I enjoyed running errands in my Mustang. But she also knew I liked to take the long way to get where I was going. Driving was still new enough to me that I enjoyed every second behind the wheel—even in traffic.

"Promise me you'll go straight there."

"Cross my heart," I told her.

She wanted me to leave at dawn, before she went off to work. If I had, the whole nasty business might have been avoided, but as it was, I slept late. The sun was already high in the sky by the time I hit the street, where the neighborhood girls had been playing hopscotch, probably since the break of dawn.

"Hey, Red Rider, we like your new wheels," the girls said as I passed them on the way to where the Mustang was parked. "Who's gonna get your bicycle now that you got a car?"

"Who says anybody's going to get it?" I told them, "Some days are bicycle days; some days are Mustang days."

I hopped into the car and little Tina Soames took a moment away from her hopscotch game to lean in the window.

"Betcha it gets stolen," she said, and smiled with a broken front tooth that would never be fixed, because her parents didn't care enough. "Betcha it gets stolen real soon."

If anybody was going to steal my car, it would be her brother, Cedric. Cedric Soames: a rich name for such a lowlife—and believe me, life didn't get any lower than him. He was a year older than me. He rarely showed at school, but he got good grades anyway, because even the teachers were afraid of him and his gang.

"So, Tina," I asked, "is that a warning, or a threat?"

She shrugged. "A little bit of both, I guess. I know you built the thing up from a pile of junk, so I would hate to see you lose it. But then again, my brother sure does bring home nice things." Then she skipped away to continue her game of hopscotch.

I started the car, listened to the purr of the engine for a few seconds, then tore out, heading across town toward Forest Boulevard, where Grandma lived. I couldn't get the thought of Cedric out of my mind. He wasn't just mean, he was unnatural—definitely one of the burned ingredients in our neighborhood melting pot. And some things are best never scraped from the bottom of the pan.

It was a hot July day. You could see steam from the morning's rain rising from the asphalt. The humidity made you feel like you were breathing bathwater, and my shirt stuck to my skin like it was painted there. I was still thinking about Cedric Soames when I came to the intersection of Andersen and Grimm—one of the busiest corners in my neighborhood, with a traffic light that always took too long to change. I sat at the intersection, waiting for a green light, when some guy dressed in rags put a squeegee to my windshield and started to wipe it clean, even though it was clean to begin with.

"Hey, man," I said through my open window. "I don't have change for you, so you might as well forget it."

"So pay me next time," he said. "For now, just consider it a public service."

The light changed, but he was still leaning over the windshield, so I couldn't pull away. Cars behind me started honking.

"Hey, what are you doing?" I yelled at him. "Can't you see the light's green?" I honked the horn. "C'mon! Out of the way!"

He leaned even farther over the hood like he was trying to look into my car, but I figured maybe he was just studying the glass, because he said, "Look at that—some bird did its business right in the middle of your windshield."

He was right—I hadn't seen it before. Must have been an owl or something big like that. Meanwhile, the cars behind me were honking like this was my fault, but what was I supposed to do, run the dude over? He finished and I looked up. The light changed from yellow to red.

"You owe me big next time, you hear?" says the beggar. And then he flashes me a smile I recognize. He had a single gold tooth—not one of the front ones, but the sharp one. His canine tooth. The one on the left.

"Marvin Flowers?" I said.

"In the flesh," he answered.

"But . . . but . . . what are you doing here?"

Marvin Flowers, or "Marvelous Marvin," as he was better known, was the best high school quarterback Madison-Manfred High had ever seen. He had left town a year before, with a college scholarship and a winning gold-toothed smile, waving good-bye to all of his friends at Mad-Man. He said he was going places.

"What are you doing here washing windows for spare change?" I asked.

"Had to drop out of college," he told me. "Family problems." The sun disappeared behind a cloud, casting a shadow over Marvin's already dark expression.

"You know," he said, his voice making me feel cold in spite of the heat, "this city can get ahold of you and pull you back no matter how hard you try to climb out. Like a grave."

It was such a weird thing to say, I laughed nervously and looked to the traffic light, which was still stuck on red, almost as if it was waiting for Marvin's signal.

What am I afraid of? I said to myself. *This guy is just a street beggar now. Feel bad for him, sure, but don't fear him.*

Then Marvin smiled again and the sun returned to its normal glare. Maybe it was just to get rid of him, or maybe I really did feel sorry for him, but whatever the reason, I reached over to the little sack next to me on the seat and pulled out a bill from my grandma's stash of "bread." To my surprise, it was a fifty. I looked in the sack and couldn't find anything smaller. There had to be thousands of dollars in there. I took a deep breath. I wasn't just bringing Grandma the bread, I was bringing her the butter, and a golden knife to spread it!

Marvin leaned into the window and raised his eyebrows. He had seen what was in the bag, too. I wanted to peel away, but still the light stayed red.

"Just something for my grandma," I told him, tossing the bag to the floor of the car.

"Very nice."

"Here." I handed him the fifty. "Great job on the window."

"Thank you very much." He pocketed it. Then, I figured out of appreciation for the fifty, he said, "You know . . . my sister likes you."

This was news to me. Marissa Flowers was in my grade, but she never looked at me twice. I, on the other hand, had looked at her a lot more than twice.

"She's got a summer job over at Stiltskin's Antiques. In fact, she's there right now, bored out of her mind, I'll bet. A visit from you would brighten up her day, I think."

"You think so?"

"I know so."

"My grandma is expecting me."

"Old people are patient," he said. "What difference is half an hour going to make? Or even an hour, for that matter?"

I guess he was right. After all, my father always said you gotta make time for the finer things in life, and Marissa Flowers was definitely one of those finer things.

"Maybe I will," I told him.

He smiled and nodded—and with his nod the light turned green. "See you around, Red."

2
THIRTEEN STEPS TO GRANDMA'S HOUSE

Stiltskin's Antiques was a little hole-in-the-wall shop. My mother used to drag me there when I was little. It was where I got my old Radio Flyer wagon, so the place wasn't all bad. As I didn't have a cell-phone habit, I couldn't call Grandma from the car, and the pay phones I passed weren't about to take a fifty-dollar bill, so I figured Grandma wouldn't mind waiting just a little while longer. She was the one who was fond of saying "all good things come to those who wait," and the sack of money was certainly a good thing.

There was a space right out in front with half an hour still on the meter. I should have found this suspicious. I should have realized there were forces conspiring, but I just figured it was my lucky day. I locked the bag of cash in my trunk and went in.

"Well, if it isn't the Red Rider," Marissa Flowers said as she saw me step in.

The place smelled like wet wood and old folks, but everything in there was beautiful. Pink and blue crystal, delicate porcelain, and of course, Marissa. She was at the cash register, polishing a tea set to perfection.

"What brings you here?" she asked, batting her eyes and tossing her long hair, which was dark with blond highlights.

I felt myself going red and hoped she didn't notice. "I need a birthday present for my mother," I told her, which wasn't a complete lie. I eventually *would* need one.

"What kind of antiques does she like?" Marissa said.

"Beats me. I don't know anything about antiques."

"Neither do I," she admitted. "When I took the job, I couldn't tell brass from bronze, or crystal from Corning Ware. But I'm learning."

She put down the silver set so gently it didn't make a sound, and then began pulling out a whole bunch of bright colorful glass vases that weren't anywhere near my price range.

"How about one of these?" she asked. "Do you like any of them?"

"Yeah, I like them all," I told her. I couldn't look in her eyes. If her brother had made it seem like the sun had stopped shining, she made it seem like the place had no roof and the sun was beating down.

Did you ever get the feeling that everything was too perfect? Like the moment was so good that something had to be wrong? Kind of like the way a fish sees that bright, shiny lure just before it chomps down and gets hauled out of the water to become someone's lunch.

"Say, I was wondering what time you get off?" I asked.

"Why?"

I shrugged and looked away. "Oh, I thought you might like to go to the multiplex and see a movie."

"With you?"

"No, with Godzilla," I said. "So, you want to come?"

"That depends. Is Godzilla paying?"

"Well," I said, "since Godzilla asked, Godzilla will pay."

Marissa laughed. "Don't worry, Red. I'll pay for myself."

My jaw almost dropped clear to the musty floor. "So that means you're going?"

"I get off at six-thirty," she told me.

"All right. See you then." I'm not the kind of guy to skip, but I have to tell you, I practically skipped out of that antique shop and into my car. As I drove off, it was as if my wheels didn't even touch the ground.

Grandma lived in the oldest part of the city. On both sides of the street were rows of dark brick homes with tall stoops. Each had thirteen steps—"like gallows," Grandma was fond of saying.

The sidewalk was all broken up, like a fun-house floor, by the roots of the hundred-year-old sycamores that arched over Forest Boulevard. They made the sun play peekaboo, painting the streets in polka dots of light. It was a great street for Halloween, because by fall, the whole street was layered in golden leaves that crunched under your feet. But now, in July, the leaves made a big green canopy, like some sort of urban rain forest.

I pulled my car into the driveway, got the money sack from the trunk, and climbed the thirteen steps to Grandma's house, holding it tightly in my hand.

As I neared the front door, a hot breeze tore through the trees, making them quiver. Something tumbled down across my hair and over my shoulder. I brushed it off, thinking at first that it was a spider, but it was only a leaf. A big, summer-green sycamore leaf.

Why had the leaf fallen? I wondered. For the slightest instant, I had the strange feeling that the trees were trying to tell me something. "Sssssssstay outsssssssssssside," their leaves rustled. "Don't sssssssstep in."

I shook off the feeling and rang the bell. No answer. I tried the bell again and still no answer.

Well, I am *late,* I thought. Maybe Grandma went out shopping. I tried the door. The knob turned, the door was unlocked. That was odd. Grandma was never one to leave her door unlocked. The neighborhood wasn't the safest. I pushed open the door and the old hinges creaked.

"Grandma, are you in there?"

I heard breathing. Faint, raspy breathing.

"Grandma?"

I stepped in, propping the door open behind me. Grandma kept her house dark. It was to keep the sun from aging the carpeting and furniture, she always said. Old venetian blinds covered every window. That and the trees outside made it always seem like night in her house. I tried a light switch, and it didn't work.

"Grandma, did you forget to pay your electric bill again?"

"Red," I heard. "Red, is that you?" Her voice sounded funny, like she had a cold. I followed her voice to the bedroom, and there she sat, in the darkness, under her covers.

"Did you bring me my bread?" she whispered.

I held up the bag.

"Good, good." She cleared her throat. "Come a little closer, my child. Let me see you."

Grandma was the only person I allowed to call me child. As I stepped closer and my eyes began to adjust to the light, I could see that her Afro, all curly and gray, was even bigger than I had last seen it.

"Man, Grandma, what big hair you have."

"The better to style with, my dear."

Her finger reached out and beckoned to me. I took another step closer. Outside the trees hissed their eerie warning, and now there was a smell in the room. It wasn't the smell of moth-balls and air freshener that usually filled her house. This smell was alive and dark. It was gamy, like the breath of a tiger after eating its kill. I took a step closer. There was a glass beside the bed filled with water and Grandma's false teeth. They were magnified by the curved glass.

"Wow, Grandma," I said. "What gnarly teeth you have."

"Better to smile at you with, my dear."

She put out her hand and patted the bed for me to sit down, but even in this dim light, I could see there was something very odd about those hands.

"My, Grandma," I said. "What hairy knuckles—"

But I didn't get the chance to finish. Suddenly Grandma

leaped off the bed, and I was pushed back against the wall. Both of her hands were around my throat. I reached up, pulled at her hair, and it came off. It was only a wig.

"Guess we're gonna have to do this the hard way!" she said, in a voice that didn't sound like my grandma at all. "Give me the money!"

I kept trying to suck air through my throat, but those strong hands had closed off my windpipe. I knew from that voice exactly who it was. Although I couldn't see his face all that well in the dim light, I knew.

Cedric Soames.

I reached out behind me, grabbed the cord to the blinds, and tugged as hard as I could. Light flooded the room. I could see his eyes now, wild and furious. I had never been this close to him, but now I could see there was definitely something inhuman about his eyes.

Other figures stepped out from behind the curtains, from the closet, and from the other rooms. There were more than I could count, because my vision was getting dim from the lack of oxygen.

I knew right away that they were the Wolves, Cedric's gang. Their trademark was an open shirt that showed off their chest hair—although most of them had to use mascara to make it look like anything. Cedric was the only really hairy one.

"Just take it," I tried to say. "Just take it."

Cedric twisted his lip into a snarling smile.

"I don't take things," he said. "But I do accept gifts. Are you giving me that money?"

Although there wasn't an ounce of me that wanted to do it,

I also didn't want to die. I let the bag slip from my hands. One of the others picked it up, and when he stood up and looked at me, I could see who it was. Marvin Flowers, gold tooth and all.

Now that I had dropped the bag, Cedric loosened his grip enough to let me gasp some air.

"Where's my grandma?" I asked.

"We ate her," said one of the other Wolves.

"Yeah," said Cedric. "I think I still have a piece of her between my teeth. Marvin, go see if there's any dental floss."

I pushed Cedric for that one. I knew he might hit me hard, but no one makes fun of my grandma like that. Especially after stealing from her.

"What did you do with her?" I demanded.

"Same thing we're gonna do with you."

Cedric looked at me angrily, but he didn't hit me. He stared at me with his nasty eyes. They were an amber brown, so light they could almost be yellow—an ugly yellow, like the stuff you cough up when you've got the flu. And smack in the middle of those ugly eyes were dark pupils that seemed to go all the way to the back of his head—and then some.

"You don't get what's happening here, do you?" Cedric growled as he held me back against the wall. He was older than me, bigger than me, and his biceps were as thick as my legs, but I didn't care.

"Yeah, I know exactly what's happening here," I growled right back at him. "You're ripping off money from a poor defenseless old lady. That's low even for a scuzzball like you."

I thought I'd get a five-knuckle brunch for that, but instead he laughed. The rest of the Wolves laughed as well, copying whatever Cedric did—as if they'd be in trouble if they didn't.

"You don't know a stinkin' thing." Then he leaned closer, whispering into my ear. "There are worse things than being robbed . . ." I could smell the sick old-meat stench on his breath, like he really *had* eaten my grandmother. ". . . worse things than dyin' even. You be a good boy, Little Red, and maybe you'll get to live awhile. Maybe you'll get to die in your own natural time."

"I'd rather die than have to stand here looking at your ugly face. Your mama should've got a refund for it when you were born."

He squeezed my throat again. "You watch yourself, Little Red Rider. You don't want to get me angry. Not today. Definitely not today."

"Why?" I dared to ask. "What makes today so special?"

"Because," said Cedric, "tonight there's a full moon."

3
▲
"THIS ISN'T EXACTLY THE DATE I HAD IN MIND"

My dad always said that belonging to a gang was a way for small-minded people to feel big. He says it works like this: You take a whole bunch of people with more attitude than brain, and maybe if you're lucky all those small brains will add up to one full brain. But I have a different theory. I think it's like multiplication, not addition. Half-a-brain times half-a-brain equals a quarter-brain. You get enough half-brains together, and you end up with cockroach intelligence. That's what I figured I had here in dealing with the Wolves.

"Take him down," Cedric shouted, now that he had the money sack in his clutches. Taking someone down usually meant killing them. Is that what they had done to Grandma? I didn't want to think about it. On Cedric's orders, Marvin Flowers grabbed me by my shirt, lifted me off the ground, and hauled me out of Grandma's room.

"What's the matter, Marvin?" I said, almost choking on my fear. "The fifty I gave you before wasn't enough? You had to take the rest? That's worse than begging for change on street corners."

"I ain't no beggar," he said, annoyed at the suggestion. "Cedric assigned me to case out cars and people at that corner. Easier to do it while I'm washing windows."

"Case them out for what?"

"For anything we decide we need."

"Like my grandmother's money?"

He snarled at that, baring that gold canine tooth of his, holding me even higher off the ground as he moved me through the house. "It's that money that saved you," he said. "Getting that blood money put Cedric in a good mood."

Saved me? I thought. *But didn't Cedric tell him to "take me down"?*

"So, you're not gonna kill me?"

"Not right now, but don't ask me about later."

I thought of saying something about his sister—about how we were supposed to go out tonight. But then I thought, what if that whole thing was a scam? What if she had been just a decoy so that the Wolves could get to Grandma's house? I'm sure that's what Marvin had intended, but was Marissa in on it, too? I silently cursed myself for allowing the Flowerses to lead me astray long enough for the Wolves to get here first.

"You don't have to listen to everything Cedric says," I told him. "Just because he's a dungworm doesn't mean you have to be."

"Cedric's right—you don't know a thing. And it's best if it stays that way."

Then he pulled open the basement door and hurled me down into darkness. I didn't even connect with the stairs—I flew all the way down until I smashed against the cold, damp concrete. I groaned as the pain in my knees, wrist, and side peaked, then faded, but it didn't go away completely. The door up above had been closed and locked before I had even hit the ground, and there was no light in the basement at all. I lay there listening to my own breathing and the creaks from the floorboards above me as the Wolves moved around, probably ransacking the house. And then across the basement I heard the *click-hiss* of a match being struck. For an instant I saw a face behind the flaring light before the match went out. I gasped.

"Grandma?"

The sulfur smell of the match overpowered the stench of age-old mildew in the basement. "Caught you, did he? Sorry about that, Red."

It *was* Grandma. No imitation this time. "Grandma, are you okay?" Just hearing her voice brought a huge wave of relief. The Wolves might have been killers, but at least they weren't killers today. My bones still hurt too much to move, so I just zeroed in on her voice across the room, and a tiny spot of orange light, not bright enough to light up her face. It was the tip of a cigarette. I didn't even know Grandma smoked.

"Been better, been worse," Grandma said. "Not my first time in the belly of the beast, if you catch my meaning."

I didn't catch her meaning at all, but that was nothing new. Grandma always lobbed out expressions that no one could catch but her.

"They get my bread?" she asked.

"Huh? Oh—the money. Yeah. I'm sorry."

"Not your fault," she said. "I should have known. That Cedric Soames is no different than his grandfather. Can't change what's in the blood."

I heard her breathe out, and the smell of the spent match was replaced by a perfumy smoke, like burning spice. It was something I'd never smelled before, and I thought I had smelled just about every kind of cigarette.

"What are you smoking, Grandma?"

"Aconitum napellus," she said. "It's a special herb some old friends taught me about a long long time ago. Nothing illegal, mind you, but highly poisonous, if you don't use it just right. I usually drink tiny bits of it as tea, but any port in a storm, if you catch my meaning," which I didn't. She took another puff and blew out the smoke in my direction. I coughed. "Like I said, can't change blood, but you can change its flavor for a time, when you need to."

I had no idea what she was talking about, but this was the third time in five minutes I had heard the word *blood*. I didn't like it.

"We'll wait down here until they go away," she said calmly. "Those boys won't bother us down here now."

"How do you know?"

"I just do."

Grandma drew in a deep breath and breathed out the smoke. "You come close to me, Red. Let the fumes soak into your clothes."

I didn't know why I'd want to do that, but I sidled up beside Grandma anyway.

"Ahh, *Aconitus napellus,*" she said, flicking ash from the tip of the cigarette. "Of course it's known by a more common name."

"What?" I asked.

Although I couldn't see her smiling in the dark, somehow I knew she was. "Wolfsbane," she said.

Three hours later the noises from upstairs stopped, and we climbed the stairs. I pried open the door with a crowbar to find the house a mess. Cans and bottles were everywhere, garbage was thrown all around. Grandma was fit to be tied.

"Those lousy, stinking sons of such-and-such," Grandma ranted. "Those boys are gonna get theirs, let me tell you. It's gonna come to them in spades, and I'll be shovelin'."

It wasn't until we were done cleaning the house that I thought to look outside. My car—the beautiful red Mustang that I had restored from a hunk of junk, my latest and greatest red set of wheels—it was gone!

"They took it!" I shouted. "They took my Mustang!" I ran outside and down the long stone stairs to the street. There wasn't a trace that I had ever parked it there. The Wolves were now riding around town in *my* car. I screamed from the pit of my stomach, stomping and punching the air.

Grandma slowly came down the steps until she stood beside me.

"We gotta go to the police!" I shouted. "We gotta report it!"

Grandma just shook her head sadly. "You can't go to the police, Red. Not when the Wolves are involved."

"But . . . but . . ."

"Trust me," she said. "Some things are simply *beyond* the police. Cedric Soames's pack is one of those things."

Although I had a mountain of stuff on my mind, I hadn't forgotten about Marissa. There was only one way to find out whether or not she was in league with her bad-boy brother. I had to show up at the antique shop, just like I had promised, and take her to the movies. I hoped she was being honest about wanting to go, now not so much because I liked her, but because it would burn Marvin's hide to know that he was responsible for his sister going out with me.

It was already late afternoon by the time I left Grandma's house. I had to take two buses to get to the antique shop—something I hated, because it reminded me that I didn't have a car anymore. The buses were late, the traffic was slow, and I didn't get there until a quarter of eight: almost sunset at this time of year. The CLOSED sign was already hanging in the window. I kicked the sidewalk in frustration. She was probably gone by now. I went to the door, but it was locked, so I went around to the back alley.

The alley was a narrow lane, unevenly paved, filled with bits of broken glass and Dumpsters that smelled like bad fish on a hot day. I knocked on the back door of the shop. To my surprise, the door opened when my knuckles hit it.

I slipped inside. "Hello?"

The lights were off, and the sun, low in the sky, shone through the front window at a crooked angle, glinting off the crystal and making the dust in the air glow like snow under a streetlight.

"Anybody here? Marissa?" Maybe she was in the bathroom. She wouldn't have left the back door unlocked if she had gone home.

No answer. In the dark corners, antique Mardi Gras masks peered out at me. A ventriloquist's dummy leered at me from a shelf, its lips twisted in a porcelain sneer. I kept thinking its eyes followed me, along with the eyes of all the other masks and little statuettes in the room.

"Marissa?" I said, getting more spooked by the minute. The sun shifted behind a building across the street, leaving the antique shop in an eerie twilight gloom. Everything was in shadows, and every shadow seemed to be moving. A jingling sound behind me rattled my nerves, and I spun. No one was there. Just a wind chime shifting slightly. Something was wrong about that, and it took me a few seconds to figure out what it was. Wind chimes move in a breeze, and there was no breeze.

Suddenly something came down on my head. A pattern of lights flashed in my eyes, kind of like seeing stars in a cartoon. There was a sharp pain in my skull, and I felt my cheek hit the floor before I even realized I had fallen down. I never really fell unconscious—I was just dazed and dizzy. I felt myself get hoisted up, and felt ropes on my hands, but my eyes were still rolling into my head from the blow, and I didn't catch sight of my attacker until the spinning world began to slow down. When it did, I found myself hog-tied to a red leather armchair that smelled of old cigar smoke, somewhere in the back of the antique shop.

Sitting in an identical chair across from me was Marissa.

"What did you do that for?"

"I think you know," she said.

I didn't know much of anything right then. That blow left me barely remembering my own name. "What did you hit me with?"

She reached over and pulled a nasty-looking rifle onto her lap. "I hit you with this rifle butt. As for the business end, you'll be meeting that in just a few minutes, I suspect."

I wanted to think she was joking, but she was serious. Deadly serious.

"This is about your brother, isn't it?"

"No. It's about you. It's about the things you do. It's about what you *are*."

"I don't know what you're talking about."

"Well, if that's true, we'll know soon enough." She looked up at a skylight above us. The sky was painted with purple-and-orange clouds. Dusk was kicking up colors and would soon be settling into night.

Marissa stood up, went off, and came back with something in her hands. There was a little table between us—cherrywood with fancy frills and clawed feet. She slammed the thing down on the table.

It was a skull. A human skull. Its empty eye sockets stared out at me. Its yellowed teeth were fixed in a snarling grin.

"What the . . ."

She sat down across from me, took the rifle, and laid it across her lap. "Now we wait."

"Do you have to leave that skull on the table staring at me? It's bad enough I have to sit here at all, why did you have to put that there?"

She didn't answer.

"This isn't exactly the date I had in mind," I told her.

She sighed. "Do I have to gag you?"

After that I kept quiet.

Slowly the clouds beyond the skylight bruised deeper, until the sky was dark. Still Marissa stared at me. Then, through a back window, a thin shaft of moonlight shone in, hitting the table. The dome of the skull glowed a faint blue in the darkness.

And what I saw then I will never forget for as long as I live.

The skull began to change.

4

THE SKULL OF
XAVIER SOAMES

'd seen strange things in my life, and heard of things stranger still, but nothing could prepare me for what happened to that skull once the moonlight touched it.

The dome began to elongate, the jaw pulled back, the nose stretched forward, and those grinning teeth changed, too. The canines lengthened and sharpened, and the eye sockets shrank until I was no longer looking at a human skull. I was looking at the skull of some hideous beast.

I stared at the skull, astonished, and when I looked up Marissa was staring at me, just as shocked—but her expression wasn't about the skull. She was shocked by me.

"Oh my gosh, Red, I'm so sorry!" She put down the rifle and came over to untie me.

"Do you mind telling me what this is all about? Am I having a hallucination? Is this a concussion from getting knocked in the head?"

"No," Marissa said as she finished untying me. "It's real. You saw what you saw."

"And what exactly did I see?"

She sighed. "It's best if you don't know. Just go home, and forget what happened here."

Sure—like I could possibly forget any of it. "I'm not going anywhere until you tell me."

She looked at me long and hard. "Once you know, it will haunt you forever. You'll go to bed thinking about it. You'll wake up thinking about it. It will fill your dreams. Are you sure you want to know?"

I nodded.

She reached down and picked up the terrible animal skull from the table. "This is the skull of Xavier Soames. Cedric Soames's grandfather."

I was never one to believe in werewolves. That was just silly stuff they showed on TV late at night to keep you awake so you'd watch the commercials. Sure, some people seemed to have more animal in them than human at times, but changing from man into beast—it just didn't happen in the world I was raised in. At least that's what I had always thought. Now I wasn't so sure. I wasn't sure about anything anymore.

"Xavier Soames was the first," Marissa told me. "The first one in our neighborhood anyway. He started a gang."

"The Wolves!"

"That was thirty years ago. But a couple of werewolf hunters came along to end the curse, and sent them all to their graves. The Wolves were gone, and for the longest time the only gang in town that people took seriously was that all-girl gang—the Crypts, I think they're called. They're not werewolves, and as far as I know, they haven't bothered anyone. The neighborhood recovered from the dark years. . . . Then, just a couple of years ago, Cedric started it up again and gathered a bunch of new members every bit as bad as the first."

"But . . . but he's not a werewolf, right? He's just pretending, right? Right?"

"Haven't you heard the stories," Marissa said, "about coyotes getting neighborhood cats and dogs? Since when have there ever been coyotes in the middle of the city?"

It was true that there had been more warnings about coyotes over the past year. And now that I thought about it, I remembered my mom always saying that when she was a kid, there were a few years when she couldn't go out at night because of them, especially when the moon was bright, and . . . I gasped as I realized what I was thinking. Not when the moon was bright, but when the moon was *full*.

"And," said Marissa, "what about all those reports about teenagers in our neighborhood running away from home?"

"So, what about it?"

"Think, Red! Those kids didn't run anywhere. Oh, maybe they tried to run, but they didn't get too far. No farther than a wolf's belly."

"No!"

"Yes! And they don't leave any evidence. Werewolves—they eat their prey, bones and all." Then she picked up the hideous wolf skull from the table. "Of course, you don't have to be afraid of old Xavier Soames here—he can't hurt you anymore.

Now I just use him as a test. You see, the moment this skull changes from human to wolf, that's the moment they all transform. That's how I know you're not one of them."

I rubbed the back of my head. A knot the size of a walnut had risen there.

"I've been trying to figure out their identities for months now, but the Wolves are very secretive. They don't make their identities known often, and when they do, it's usually the last thing that person sees. Cedric's the only one we know for sure."

"But I saw some of them!" I said. "I can identify—" Then something suddenly dawned on me.

She must have seen the way my jaw dropped halfway to the ground. "What's wrong?"

"Your brother . . ." I almost didn't tell her, but I knew I had to. It was too serious not to tell.

"My brother what?"

"Your brother's one of them."

She stepped back from me and looked at me in anger, as if I had slapped her right across the face. "Don't you say that! Don't even think it! He'd never be one of them! Never!"

"But I saw him!"

"You take it back! You're lying just to get back at me for hitting you! You take it back!"

But I shook my head. It hurt my brain to shake it. "He came to my grandma's house with the rest of them this morning. They stole the money I brought for her. And then they stole my car."

She sat down in the leather chair, trying to sort it out, trying to deny what I was telling her. "Maybe Cedric's just making him pay back a favor. He does that, you know. Just because Cedric's got my brother jumping through hoops doesn't mean he's one of them. I bet he'll get away, and tell me all about it the second he does."

I thought about that nasty look on Marvin's face. He sure looked like one of them to me.

"Maybe you're right, and maybe you're wrong," I told her. "Either way, it's not safe to be out there now." I looked at the skull she held. I did not want to see the face of any creature that owned a skull like that.

"I don't get to be safe," she said. "Wolf hunters never do. And now that you know, you don't get to be safe, either. We can't do this alone—we're gonna need some help."

"So you're just gonna go to the police with werewolf stories?"

"Who said anything about the police? Thirty years ago, there were two werewolf hunters who rid the town of the curse the first time. I've been trying to track them down, but they disappeared. Some people say they died along with Xavier Soames, but others say they just went into hiding."

And then something clicked in my mind.

"My grandmother knew them! She said some old friends taught her to use wolfsbane!"

Marissa's eyes sparkled. "That's the best lead I've gotten yet! Let's find out what she knows!"

She went to the back door, pushed it open, then hesitated at the threshold. "The Wolves could be anywhere," she said. "Just around the corner, or clear across town. There's no way to know."

"Well," I said, "I guess going to the movies tonight is out, huh?"

She laughed at that. It was good that we could still laugh. Far off I heard something howl to the moon, and although it was a chilling, awful sound, I was relieved that it was so far away.

"Marissa," I asked, because I simply needed to know, "what made you think I was a werewolf?"

She looked at me a good long while before she answered. One side of her face was lit by the soft light of the room, and the other side of her face was lit by pale moonlight. My face must have looked the same to her. Half-warm, half-cold.

"You fit the profile, Red. You're restless—a little impulsive, maybe. It made me think there might be a little bit of animal in you."

I grinned. "Maybe there is," I said with a wink. I was just joking, but Marissa didn't laugh.

5
▲
MAKING
MISCHIEF

They lived just around the corner," Grandma told Marissa and me as she poured us cups of scalding-hot wolfsbane tea. "When things got bad, they taught us how to brew wolfsbane—strong enough to keep the wolves away, but not strong enough to kill you when you drank it. She spooned a heavy dose of honey into each of our cups. "There. Try that."

I stirred and took a sip. It tasted a lot better than the wolfsbane cigarette had smelled. It tasted like jasmine and mint.

Marissa tried her tea, grimaced, and added more honey. "What do you remember about them?"

Grandma shrugged. "They were just a friendly couple. Quiet. You'd never guess they were werewolf hunters. When they finally put Xavier's gang down, they just disappeared."

"Any pictures of them?" I asked. Photography was Grandma's hobby. No one ever escaped her lens.

She just shook her head sadly. "They were camera shy. If a camera came out, they made themselves scarce. I suppose I understand why. They were only safe as long as they were anonymous."

"Would you recognize them if you saw them again?" I asked.

Grandma sighed. "Thirty years changes people. I can't say I would."

Marissa stood and began to pace the room. "If we don't even know what they look like, how can we find them?"

"The medallion," said Grandma.

"Huh?"

"One of them wore a medallion—very scarred, very old. Bronze, I think it was. Find the medallion, and you'll find them."

"Yeah, like that's gonna happen," I said. "How are we going to track down a medallion?"

I reached to pour myself another cup of tea, but Grandma stopped me.

"Careful," she said. "One cup is plenty. As long as it stays in our blood, it should keep the werewolves away." Then she turned to Marissa. "Tell me, dear, how did you come by the skull of Xavier Soames?"

Marissa glanced around as if the walls might have ears, then spoke in a low whisper. "It was my uncle who got it," she said. "He's the one who told me about Xavier Soames, and how the Wolves had terrorized the neighborhood. It made him a little bit crazy, I think. For as long as I can remember, he's been very superstitious—carrying rabbit's feet, avoiding ladders, that sort of thing. He taught me all he knew about werewolves. He had read that the best way to keep evil spirits from coming back was to make mischief with their bones."

"What kind of mischief?" I asked.

"Moving the bones around in the grave, that sort of thing."

I swallowed hard. Digging up a grave, opening a coffin, and shifting bones was not the kind of mischief I'd ever want to get into.

"My uncle snuck into the graveyard late one night, just before the moon rose, and dug old Xavier up. It had been only a year, but there wasn't much left of him but crusty bones."

"Makes sense," Grandma said. "The earth is quick to consume the flesh of things that ain't natural."

"Anyway," continued Marissa, "he began to do what he came there to do, moving the bones and all, and then the moon rose. At that moment, right before his eyes, the bones began to change. Every single human bone transformed into the bone of a wolf. It scared him half out of his mind—he thought the bones themselves would reassemble and attack him. But they didn't."

"So not even the bones of a werewolf can resist the call of a full moon," Grandma said with a shiver. "That's more than I ever wanted to know."

"Before he closed the coffin and filled in the grave, he took the skull. He's kept it locked in a chest ever since, afraid to take it out, but afraid to get rid of it, too."

"Where's your uncle now?" I asked. "Maybe he can lead us to the hunters."

Marissa shook her head. "Once he realized that Xavier's grandson was also a werewolf and was gathering a new gang, he left town. He gave me the skull before he left to warn me. The first time I saw the change myself, it scared me half out of my mind, but pretty soon I realized I could use the skull kind of like a wolf clock. All I have to do is look at that skull to know when the werewolves are out. And of course, I can use it to put people like Red here to the test."

"Very clever," Grandma said, but before Marissa could feel too proud of herself, she added, "but you're a fool for carrying it around so people can see. All it takes is one member of the pack to report back to Cedric, and they won't even wait for the full moon to put you on the menu."

Marissa was a little hurt by the reprimand. "My brother looks out for me."

Grandma tossed a sour look toward her. "Marvin? He's one of them! He was right there next to Cedric when he threw me in the basement."

"And stole the money from me," I added.

"No. If he was one of them, I'm sure I'd know. He's gotten in over his head maybe, but I'm sure he hasn't been 'made' yet."

"'Made'?" I asked.

"When you join the Wolves, you don't become a werewolf right away," Marissa explained. "You've got to show your loyalty, and when Cedric thinks you're ready, he bites you, and once he does, there's no turning back. You're a werewolf."

"Does Marvin know about the skull?" I asked.

"I never showed it to him." Marissa began to pace as she thought about her brother. "Marvin has never liked Cedric—it doesn't make sense that he'd want to join the Wolves. He's got to be working some angle—trying to trick them into telling him their secrets, or trying to expose them, or something. Whatever it is, he can't really be one of them." I could see that the more she talked, the more she convinced herself she was right. "I know he helped steal your money . . . but I also know in my heart that I can trust him."

Well, I wasn't about to tell her any different—after all, she loved her brother, whether he deserved that love or not.

Grandma, on the other hand, spoke her mind plain and clear. "I don't trust him as far as I could kick him, and neither should you. Trust doesn't help you survive at a time like this."

But Marissa shook her head. "Trust is the *only* thing that helps you survive," she said. The two of them stared each other down.

"You're a foolish girl."

"And you're a suspicious old woman!" Marissa said.

"So, we've got a little trust and a little suspicion," I said, trying to referee before they got too angry at each other. "Maybe having both is a good thing." I turned to Marissa. "Marvin doesn't have to know everything you do, does he?"

Marissa sighed and shook her head. That seemed to settle Grandma a bit. "The only ones I'll trust are those hunters," Grandma said.

"Will you trust me, Grandma?" I asked.

I couldn't see her eyes behind her glasses, which had fogged up from the steam rising from her mug. "Of course, Red. Of course."

We stayed over at Grandma's that night, since the moon was still full. Marissa told her parents she was staying with a friend, and mine were thrilled when I called to tell them I was spending some quality time with Grandma. When the sun rose, Marissa and I took the Avenue C bus, sitting silently together in the back. Only after she rang the bell for her stop did she turn to me. "Last night was the third night of the full moon, so we won't have to face any wolves until next month."

But I shook my head. "We'll still have to face wolves," I told her. "They'll just be human ones."

"True enough."

I pounded my fist into my hand with such force my palm stung. A sudden fury raged in me that I couldn't put down. "I could take on Cedric right now."

"You gotta be patient," Marissa said. "Being reckless right now will get you killed."

I opened my mouth to argue, but before I could, she closed her hand gently over my fist. Then she thought for a moment. "Live by your impulses, and you'll be just like them. You're better than that, aren't you, Red?"

I couldn't answer her. Partly because I couldn't stop staring at her hand on mine, but also because I didn't know.

When I got home, Dad was gone—he was on one of his twelve-hour shifts—but Mom was still getting ready to leave for the day.

"It was nice of you to stay over with Grandma last night," she said. "She gets lonely in that house all by herself. You're a good grandson, Red."

The biggest problem with my mom is she can read me like a *TV Guide*. All she's gotta do is look at me to know whether it's drama or comedy. Today, I guess the *Guide* told her I was tuned into a horror marathon. She pursed her lips, read me a bit further, and said, "All right, what's wrong?"

I sighed, and tried to figure out what I could get away with telling her. For a second split finer than a neck hair, I thought of telling her everything. That the gang that called themselves the Wolves really were, and they were feeding on innocent townsfolk every full moon. But my parents weren't exactly the type of people I could talk to about this. My dad was a para-medic; he saw life and death every day, and nothing in between. To him there were neither curses nor miracles, only timing and triage. As for Mom, she was getting a degree in architecture. Her world was all lines and angles on a blueprint. Even in her religious beliefs she went straight by the book. For her there was no thinking outside of the lines. No, I couldn't let them know, but I couldn't lie either. I couldn't tell her Saturday-morning cartoons, when the *TV Guide* on my face said *Creature Feature*.

"My Mustang got stolen," I said. It was true, and it was hor-rific, at least to me.

"Oh, Red," she said. "And you just finished working on it!"

"I never should have left it parked on the street," I said, my anger real. "I should have put it in Grandma's garage."

"We'll go to the police," she told me. "We'll make a report."

"I already did," I told her. "With Grandma."

I knew she'd call Grandma to talk about it, but I also knew that Grandma was quick enough to play along and not give away the truth.

"You'll get it back," Mom said. "I know you will."

"So do I," I told her. She hugged me, gave me some bus fare, then left. Once she was gone, I took a few sprigs of wolfs-bane from my pocket, made myself a cup of tea just like

Grandma taught me, and drank it down to the bitter, weedy dregs. Then I went out looking for Cedric Soames.

Cedric's little sister was at her usual spot, jumping rope with her friends, doing it so well, you'd think double Dutch should be an Olympic sport. When she saw me signal to her, she hopped out of the spinning circle of ropes and skipped over to me.

"Cedric said you'd be coming by," she said, flashing me her ugly smile. "He said to warn you not to look for him and his friends, or he might have to do something nasty."

"Where is he?"

"Driving around in our new car." Tina popped a pink bubble that stuck to her face. "It's nice. But I guess you already know how nice it is."

I huffed angrily, and she wrinkled her nose. "You got bad breath. Smells like you been chewing crabgrass."

I blew more air in her direction, wondering if Tina might be a werewolf, too.

"Ewww," she said. "Go suck an Altoid."

Yes, I had to admit, wolfsbane breath was pretty gross—but the fact that she still stayed there after smelling it meant Cedric hadn't given his little sister the bite.

"You tell your brother he's gonna pay for that car with silver."

"What's that supposed to mean?"

"He'll know."

I walked off, and she returned to her friends, but when I looked back, it seemed to me that she couldn't pick up the rhythm of the ropes no matter how hard she tried.

For three days, rather than taking the bus, I rode my old red Schwinn around town, always imagining I'd see my Mustang just around the corner. I wasn't quite sure what I'd do if I came across Cedric, so perhaps it was best I didn't find it.

Marissa and I worked day and night to track down the werewolf hunters. It was a dangerous business, because if word of what we were doing got back to Cedric, we'd be history.

Most of Marissa's time was spent at the library, scouring old newspapers and public records for clues. She discovered the dates and names of people who'd gone missing. She found out which homes were bought and sold during those dark times, and even found out where some of the sellers moved to—hoping that it would lead us to the hunters.

Me, I didn't have the patience for that sort of thing. I had to be on the prowl, so I took to the streets in Grandma's neighborhood. I started mowing lawns and doing other favors for some of Grandma's older neighbors, getting them to like me and trust me enough—and for me to trust *them* enough—to ask them questions.

"I've been in this very house for thirty-six years," one old-timer said as I helped him take his trash cans out to the curb.

"Wow, that's a long time to live in one place," I said . . . then I started meandering around to the real questions. "I hear rumors about weird things that went on way back then."

He looked down into his trash can like there was something

interesting in there, but I knew he was just avoiding my gaze. "Depends on what you mean by weird."

"Weird like a couple of hunters."

"Nothing weird about hunters. Lots of folks hunt."

"Well, I hear these hunters didn't exactly hunt deer. Or so I heard."

He still stared into the trash can, so I pushed just a little further.

"It makes me wonder where they might be now."

"Dead, I expect," the old man said. "Hunters of that nature don't live very long."

"But if they are alive, I wonder where they might be . . . and how a person might be able to get them a message. . . ."

The old man backed away from the trash can and waved his hand in front of his nose. "Whew, what a stench." He covered the can with the lid. "Good thing about bad rubbish is you can make the stench go away just by covering it up. It never comes back as long as you keep a tight lid on it."

"Maybe so," I told him. "But sometimes the really bad stenches come back."

He looked at me then. We both knew we weren't talking about trash. He reached into his pocket and pulled out a couple of crumpled dollar bills, holding them out to me. "Thanks for your help."

I didn't take his money. "My pleasure."

I turned to go, but before I got too far, he called to me.

"If you talk to the right people, maybe your message will get through."

I turned to ask him who might the right people be—but he had already gone inside.

There were a few more folks on the street who had been around for thirty years or more, but they were all like the old man—afraid to talk, like maybe just talking about it would bring the bad times back. Still, I did find out some things. Like how every house on the block had once had silver doorknobs. And how the local playground had become overgrown with wolfsbane that someone had planted years ago. That is, until someone mysteriously torched it just a few months back. Then there was this one crazy old woman who showed me a little lock of hair she kept in a jar of formaldehyde.

"It came from a werewolf," she told me, her eyes big as golf balls. "It turns to wolf fur on the full moon."

The old woman also said it belonged to Frank Sinatra, but I had serious doubts.

It was as I rode down Bleakwood Avenue on my way to meet Marissa at the library that I heard the threatening roar of a motorcycle beside me. Before I knew what happened, a Harley, black as a moonless night, cut me off, clipped my front wheel, and sent me flying head over heels onto the pavement, skinning my palms and knees.

I looked up, fully ready to battle whoever it was, but was stopped by what I saw. There was a black medallion hanging around the cyclist's neck, dangling heavily against his leather jacket. I tried to get a glimpse of his face, but his visor was as dark as the motorcycle. Still, I could tell he was looking straight at me. This hadn't been an accident.

"I've been looking for you," I said, picking myself off the ground. "The Wolves are back. We need your help."

He didn't respond right away. He just stood there, sizing me up. And then a harsh whisper came from beneath his visor.

"Stay out of this!"

Then he gunned the Harley and disappeared down Bleakwood as quickly as he had come.

6

WICKED as
a WOLF

It's all for the best, I suppose." Grandma had me sitting up on the dining-room table as she tended to my palms and knees. The stinging antiseptic solutions smelled worse than wolfsbane. It made me wonder what evil doctor decided that if it hurts it must be cleaning the wound. "At least we know the hunters are back, and on top of things."

"I only saw one of them," I told her.

"Well, one's better than none."

"Ow!"

"Now don't be a baby. It's not that bad."

Marissa, sitting across the room, snickered, so I bit my lip to keep myself from whining. I was never a very good patient.

"Does it hurt worse than when I clobbered you over the head?" Marissa asked.

"I don't know," I told her. "You knocked me half-unconscious, so I didn't feel much of anything at the time."

She snickered again. *Fine*, I thought. *Let her. She was just jealous because she hadn't been the one to find the hunter.*

"If he thinks I'm just gonna back off and let Cedric Soames get away with stealing my wheels, he's wrong."

Grandma slapped a Band-Aid over one knee and moved to the other one. "You got a foolish streak in you, Red."

"What's that supposed to mean?"

"It means that you should back off and leave wolf hunting to those who know how. I'm sure you'll get your car back in time. Now hold still."

"Marissa and I can help the hunters."

"Yeah," Marissa said. "We can be kind of like . . . apprentices."

Grandma looked at my hands, which weren't scratched enough for Band-Aids, and shook her head. "They gave you a warning today. You keep sticking your nose in this, you're gonna wind up part of the problem."

"Cedric took your money, and my car. I can't just sit around and wait for someone else to take care of it. That's just not the way I'm built."

"You keep it up, and you won't be 'built' at all. You'll be in pieces. The Wolves will see to that."

I squirmed a bit at the thought and hopped off the table.

"There," Grandma said. "Good as new. Now you both get on home—and Red, don't you dare tell your parents what you've been up to."

We left without another word about my run-in with the hunter—but even before we reached the bottom of Grandma's long stone stoop, Marissa and I were already making plans.

"You still remember it?" Marissa asked.

I nodded. "Four-L-Y-C-Nine," I told her. I had burned that license plate number into my memory as the black Harley had sped off. It wasn't something I was going to forget anytime soon—but it was also something I wasn't gonna tell Grandma. Some things she just didn't need to know.

"I've got an aunt who works at the Thirty-fifth Precinct," Marissa said. "She could run the license plate and tell us who owns that motorcycle. We'll have their name, address, everything we'd ever want to know about them."

"What do you think the hunters'll do when we show up at their door?"

Marissa grinned. She was up for this just as much as I was. "Maybe they'll be impressed that we actually managed to track them down. But then again, maybe they'll leave motorcycle tread marks on our faces."

"One thing's for sure," I told her. "If they don't want us to be part of the problem, then they'd better find a way to make us part of the solution."

After all that riding around town looking for my Mustang, it finally turned up just a block from my front door.

It was the very next day. Marissa was off trying to get her aunt to trace that license plate, and I was walking back from the supermarket with a bag of groceries for my mom, trying to pretend, if only for a few minutes, that this was an ordinary summer.

Then a glint of red caught my eye, and I saw it, right there at the intersection. My Mustang, with Cedric Soames behind the wheel. Even though I knew he had taken it, and knew he must have been driving it, seeing it with my own eyes made me crazy. It made my blood boil so hot, my brain stopped working right. The light changed, and he floored it, like he was drag-racing everyone in the city. It wasn't just him in the car. There were at least five or six other guys with him, squeezed in.

I dropped the groceries and took after them on foot. I didn't have a chance of keeping up with them, but the traffic and lights slowed them down just enough for me to keep the car in my sights. I was in pretty good shape, but not for this kind of sprinting. I must have rammed into half a dozen people on the sidewalk. What would I do if I caught up with him? I didn't know. He had almost killed me before. Closed off my windpipe until I had almost blacked out. All I knew was that I couldn't stop chasing him as long as I had that car in my sights.

He made a left turn far up ahead, and when I got to the cor-ner, I thought for sure he'd be long gone. But I was wrong. My red Mustang was parked on the street, just a block ahead. Cedric and the others weren't in it, but it was no mystery where they had gone. The car was parked in front of the Cave—a sleazy pool hall where my mama told me never to go. Well, she wasn't here now.

My heart pounding and my head light from all that running, I stormed toward the car. I'd never hot-wired a car before, but I knew how it was done. Usually people do it when they're stealing the car. I'd be doing it to get my car back.

I got close enough to see my reflection in the sideview mir-ror, when out of nowhere something dark and sleek pulled in front of me. A jet-black Harley. How did the hunter know I was here? Had he been following me? I tried to get around him, but he rolled his bike forward to block me.

"All I want is my car," I told him. "Why can't you just leave me alone?"

Then came that same hoarse whisper I had heard the day before. Only this time it said, "Get on."

I shook my head so hard I felt my brain rattle. "After what you did to me yesterday, there ain't nothing you can say that'll get me on that motorcycle."

And then the hunter flipped up the visor that hid his face. "Red, you are one stubborn little cuss."

Whatever I was feeling just a second before was blown so far away, I couldn't even remember it.

"Grandma?!"

"That's right. Now get your butt on my Harley, before any of those Wolves see us."

I was too stunned to do anything but obey. I hopped on behind Grandma, she popped a wheelie, and we burned rubber all the way to her house.

I suppose all the signs had been there: She knew all about wolfsbane, and more about Xavier Soames and what happened thirty years ago than anyone else. Still, the concept that my sweet old grandma was a werewolf hunter was just too much to wrap my mind around.

"Not just me," she said, once we got to her house. "Your grandpa was, too."

Grandpa had died long before I was born. Looking at all the photos of the two of them around the house, I couldn't imagine him hunting wolves any more than I could picture Grandma doing it.

Grandma went to the bathroom and picked out her helmet hair until it was a full gray Afro once again. She caught my dazed look in the mirror. "Surprised I have a secret side, Red?"

"I guess I always thought of you as the bingo type, not the wolf-hunter type."

She let out a deep, hearty laugh. Then she glanced at the Band-Aids that still covered my knees. "Sorry about yesterday," she said. "I only meant to scare you, not knock you off your bike. Guess my riding skills aren't what they used to be."

I thought of the way she wove in and out of traffic as we rode home today. "You're pretty good, if you ask me." And then I added, "Maybe you could let me take it out next time."

She didn't answer, but she didn't need to. The look on her face told all. I didn't ask again.

A heavy pounding on the front door nearly scared me out of my skin. For a split second I thought the Wolves had followed us here, but it was just Marissa. She had this paleness about her, and wide eyes, like she had been doing some mischief with bones herself.

"Red, I know who the hunter is. You're not gonna believe it."

But when she saw Grandma, still in her leather pants and jacket, Marissa realized I already knew.

"You're both too clever for your own good," Grandma said, shaking her head in both exasperation and admiration. "Running a check on my license plate!"

"If we could do it, Grandma, don't you think the Wolves can, too?"

"It's no secret to them, Red," she told me. "They've always known."

Now that I thought about it, it made sense. Now I understood why Cedric was always so nasty to me—and why he seemed to have a grudge against her the day he stole her money. Then something came back to me. "Blood money. The Wolves called the money Cedric stole from you blood money. Why?"

"Because Cedric's a fool. He thinks we killed wolves for reward money. The truth is, people did give us money after we got rid of Xavier and his pack. We didn't ask for it, but they gave it to us anyway. Envelopes were slapped into our palms or slipped under our door. That was the bread I've been hiding all these years, the bread Cedric stole." And then she let loose a sneaky little laugh. "If he had any sense, he would have killed me right there in my basement, instead of letting the smell of wolfsbane keep him away. See, to Cedric I wasn't worth his trouble. He thinks I'm too old and feeble to be a threat to him—and that will be his downfall."

It was all coming together for me now. Marvin had been hanging out at that intersection, casing cars for things to steal—it was bad luck all around that I got caught at that particular traffic light on that particular day. But then again, maybe it wasn't luck at all. Maybe it was fate. The second Marvin told Cedric it was me—the wolf hunter's grandson—taking a big bag of cash to my grandmother, Cedric wasted no time in getting to Grandma's house before I did.

Marissa pulled her chair closer to Grandma's. "Will you tell us everything you know?"

Grandma looked at us and sighed. "I suppose I have apprentices now whether I want them or not." She went to a bureau that held dozens of photo albums. She was a photographer, after all, so photos filled every nook and cranny of her place. As a little kid, I had been through just about all of those albums. They were filled with pictures of her with Grandpa, and of their trips to strange and faraway places. But today, Grandma pulled out a photo album from the bottom of the lowest drawer. This one was full of werewolves, and of her and Grandpa's efforts as werewolf hunters. The pictures of the wolves were all taken with a telephoto lens from a safe distance, some with special film to catch them in the dark. The grainy images of snarling beasts were more disturbing than anything I had seen in my sixteen years. They didn't quite look like natural wolves, but like something almost prehistoric. Like a cross between bear and wolf, but with teeth sharp as a shark's. It was horrifying. It was fascinating. My eyes were drawn to each of those pictures, and I couldn't look away.

"We used these photos to identify them," Grandma said. "There's something about the eyes, the hair color, and the set of the jaw that doesn't change. Once we had a good picture of them in werewolf form, it was easier to figure out their human identities." She pointed to one particularly nasty-looking wolf. "That was Xavier."

I couldn't look at the picture for long. I couldn't get the feeling out of my mind that he was glaring back at me.

"Grandma, why don't you tell us how it happened the first time, and how you beat Xavier and his gang."

Grandma took a moment to look both of us in the eyes. "I thought it would be a story I would take with me to my grave. I wish I could have, but seeing how the evil's back just as strong as before, it's time the story was told."

Grandma pulled a loose brick from her fireplace, and from behind it took out a music box. "I've always kept this at hand," she said. "Just in case." She opened the lid of the music box, and it played "Amazing Grace." There wasn't any jewelry in its red velvet lining. Instead there were bullets. Silver ones. They were tarnished to the point of being almost black, but you could still tell they were silver. I found myself backing away at the sight of them, and I almost tripped over the little table behind me.

"It's true, then," I said. "Silver bullets kill werewolves!"

"It's simple science," Grandma said. "Werewolves are allergic to certain metals. They have a violent reaction to silver. Get some silver wedged in their body, and the allergic reaction kills them in less than a minute. The problem for their prey is surviving during that last minute. That's why bullets work best. You can get them from a distance, and run away safely." And then she got sad. Thoughtful. "Your grandfather and I— we knew what was going on in town. No one else wanted to admit it. No one else dared to believe it. So we did research. We traveled the world, digging through crumbling books in old libraries to learn all we could. All the details. How fast does a werewolf run? How deep does a bite have to be before they pass the curse on to you?"

"How deep?" I asked.

"Not deep at all," said Marissa, giving me a smug smile. "I've been doing research on lycanthropism, too."

"Huh?"

"Lycanthropism," said Grandma. "That's just a fancy word for the werewolf curse. But really, it's nothing more than a supernatural virus. It gets passed on in the saliva, like rabies. If a bite breaks the skin, there's a pretty good chance you've got it."

I shivered.

"After your grandpa and I learned all there was to learn, we came back. We brewed ourselves a wolfsbane cologne and wore it everywhere we went, keeping track of the people who avoided us because of the smell. To be double sure, we went to their homes every full moon, to see if they were there or not. The ones who were never home we knew were werewolves.

"Then one full moon, we went out on our motorcycles, and went after them one by one. Xavier was the hardest. He always kept himself shielded by the pack. He'd let all the others take the silver bullets meant for him. Selfish to the last."

"But in the end, you got him," I said.

"Yes, we did, Red." But she didn't say any more about it.

It was all too hard to take. Being deaf, dumb, and blind would be better than knowing the truth. These were dark days, getting darker by the minute, and I didn't even want to think about the nights. I looked to Marissa, who seemed almost hypnotized by the sight of that little musical jewelry box. On the cover was a mountain lit by a full moon. I opened it to the sound of the innocent music, and the sight of the not-so-innocent silver bullets.

"I've never used a gun, Grandma," I said. "I don't ever want to." Once, when I was little, I saw a man get shot. It happened right in front of me, on the street. Ever since then, you could say guns and me didn't get along. My dad calls it "ballistiphobia," but I call it just plain hatred. Either way, I didn't know if I'd ever be able to touch a gun, much less fire one. I guess

Grandma understood, because she took the music box from me and gently closed it.

"I don't blame you, Red. I don't blame you at all. You've got a decent heart," she said, although I wasn't sure whether or not I really did. She put the box away, and hid it behind the loose bricks again. "Different times call for different weapons."

Marissa rolled her eyes. "C'mon," she said. "You gotta kill werewolves with silver bullets. Everyone knows that."

But Grandma shook her head. "If there's one thing I learned in all of this, it's that instinct counts for a lot. If Red's instinct is to stay away from bullets, then maybe he should stay away from them."

I turned to Marissa. "What does your instinct tell you?"

Marissa looked at me, then at Grandma, and closed her eyes, going deep into herself, I guess, to tug at some of those instincts. She took a deep breath, and another, then she opened her eyes.

"It seems to me my instincts are telling me only one thing . . . that Cedric Soames is going to be harder to defeat than his grandfather."

There are werewolf legends, and there are werewolf facts. Grandma knew the difference, and that night, until the sun made a lonely appearance on the horizon, she gave us a crash course in the Lycanthropic sciences, as she called it.

On the power of the moon, she told us this: "The full moon ain't an exact sort of thing. The phase of the moon is always changing slightly. For three days, the moon is full enough to boil the blood and make a man turn wolf. The second day the curse is at its strongest, and the higher the moon is in the sky, the more deadly the wolf."

On werewolf appetites, she told us this: "In human form, they can eat anything humans eat, although they're partial to meat. In wolf form, they're driven to eat their weight in meat each night, and it must be the meat of a fresh kill."

On the mind of the werewolf, she told us this: "The mind of a human infected with the werewolf curse doesn't always start off being evil, but the way I see it, a person turns evil real quick."

On werewolf redemption, she told us this: "Ain't no such thing. No antidote, no remedy, and no turning back. Only way to save a werewolf's soul is to end its misery, and hope the good Lord truly does have infinite mercy."

And of our chances, she told us this: "We all have to die someday. Let's hope we die as humans."

By dawn, my eyelids felt as heavy as the boughs on her tree-lined street, but a plan had already started forming in my mind. Marissa went home, and I closed my eyes to take a quick nap— but when I woke up, it was already late afternoon. Grandma was still sleeping. I didn't wake her. Instead I slipped out and set a scheme in motion. It would take everything I had inside me to pull it off, and now I was restless as a caged animal, eager to get started. My plan was twisted and nasty and clever and cruel. I left that morning with a grin on my face, feeling as wicked as a wolf.

7

THE BACK ROOM
THAT DIDN'T EXIST

My Mustang was parked near the Cave again. Cedric, in his arrogance, was making no attempt at hiding it, as if he were taunting me. Taking a deep breath, I opened the door to the old pool hall and stepped inside.

The place was true to its name: dark, dingy, and smelling of stale cigar smoke and spilled beer. The pool hall was empty except for the overweight manager, who stood behind a counter, yakking on the phone. Even though I saw no customers, I heard the crack of billiard balls somewhere deep in the recesses of the place. My heart began to race, and I had to take a few deep breaths to get it under control.

The manager hung up the phone and plodded out from behind the counter. "We don't open till five," he said.

"Sounds like your back room's open."

"I ain't got a back room."

Again I heard the crack of the balls being hit from the back room that didn't exist. I grinned at him, and the manager sighed. "Listen, I don't want any trouble."

"You've already got trouble back there," I told him. "A little more won't make a difference."

Still, he didn't let me pass. He just stood there, wide as a wall, leaving no way for me to squeeze past him. I wasn't about to give up. The only way he was going to get rid of me would be to pick me up and throw me out bodily, and if he tried, I wouldn't make it easy.

Then, from the shadowy threshold of the back room, came a voice.

"Cedric says it's okay."

I recognized the voice as Loogie Stefano's, a kid I knew from school—that is, until he dropped out last semester. His real name was Luigi, but an endless stuffy nose had earned him the name Loogie.

The manager stepped aside. "Welcome to the Cave," he said. "The management cannot be held responsible for injuries or death."

By the time I reached the back room, my eyes had adjusted to the dim light. There were about a dozen of them there—some faces I recognized, some I didn't. I realized I had no idea how big Cedric's gang was. Was this most of them, or just a small handful? Were there dozens and dozens of them around town that nobody knew about? I didn't see Marissa's brother, Marvin, there, and that was just as well.

When they saw me, they all looked at one another. Could it be that they were a little bit scared of me? Or maybe they were scared of what Cedric might do to me. Either way, I felt like I had some kind of power in the situation.

Cedric was at a pool table, ignoring me. He kept shooting until he missed. Then he finally looked at me. "If you got business here, spit it out. Otherwise, get lost."

I held back an urge to go postal on him for stealing my car—but I knew that would just get me a one-way ticket to the hospital, or worse, the morgue. I had to play this like a game of pool, cleverly banking my intentions off the sides.

"I know all about you, Cedric Soames," I told him. "I know all about the 'Wolves,' and what you really are."

Cedric returned to his game. "So what are you gonna do about it?"

"Who says I'm going to do anything? There's a roomful of you, and only one of me."

He sank the six ball in a side pocket. "Then why are you here?"

I didn't answer. Instead I threw a set of keys onto the table. They hit the cue ball and knocked it to the side. "These are the spare keys to the Mustang," I said. "I got no use for them, seeing as I don't have the car anymore."

Cedric was not expecting this. He looked at the keys suspiciously, like they might blow up in his face. We both stood there on either side of the pool table, the keys between us.

"Go on, take them," I said. "It's not like they're made of silver."

He scowled at me and slowly came around the table toward me, like a wild animal stalking his prey. Part of me wanted to turn and run, but a bigger part of me wanted to stand my ground.

When he got to me, he sniffed the air around me, once, twice, three times.

"I smell fear," he said with a quiet intensity. "But not nearly enough."

I sniffed the air around him. "I won't tell you what I smell." It was something like a locker room, and something like a zoo. I'm sure he knew it. I'm sure he was even proud of it.

"You should be wetting your pants in terror, Little Red, but you're not." And then he grinned. "You're just full of surprises." He reached out his hand. I thought he was going to hit me, but instead, he leaned over the pool table, scooped up the car keys, and slipped them into his pocket. Then he turned to Loogie. "Bring Red a cue stick, and rack them up for a new game."

Loogie sucked up some snot and did what he was told.

"If you win, I let you live," said Cedric. "If you lose, I get to kill you any which way I like."

"What if I don't want to play?"

He smiled, but it looked more like an animal baring its teeth. "Not an option."

With Cedric's whole pack between me and the door, I didn't have much of a choice. I was a pretty lousy pool player, but I could put on a good show, slamming the balls hard, once in a while sinking them into a pocket I wasn't aiming for. The others watched our game, grunting their approval each time Cedric sank a ball and sneering each time I missed. For a few minutes I let myself get so absorbed in winning that game, I had forgotten why I had come, and what I intended to do. *The plan, the plan,* I told myself. Even though my life was on the line, I had to get back to the plan.

"My grandma's preparing to hunt you down," I told him.

"Tell me something I don't already know."

"You tell me something first," I said. "Tell me why you let me and my grandma live."

Silence from the whole gang. Cedric only shrugged. "We didn't let you live. Little kids and old women just aren't worth the time it would take to get rid of."

"Yeah, and after we threw youse down there, the basement reeked of wolfsbane," said Klutz McGinty, who was about as stupid as he was clumsy. "Ain't no way we was goin' down there after that!" Cedric threw him a look that could have spoiled milk, and Klutz looked down at his oversize feet, shutting up.

"I think you've got a much better reason for letting us live," I said. "A reason that you're not telling anyone."

"And what might that be?"

"Revenge."

Cedric kept his expression cold and hard to read. "Keep talking," he said.

"You could have just taken the money, but you didn't—you took my car as well. When you took my car, you knew I'd come looking for you. You *wanted* me to find you. You even parked it out on the street to make sure I would."

By now the others had uncrossed their arms, and had moved a little closer, listening intently.

"You *wanted* me to come," I said, "because you figured you could get me to turn. You could convince me to join the Wolves. And wouldn't that be the ultimate revenge on my grandma? Taking me in, and turning me into . . . one of you."

Looking at Cedric, I couldn't tell whether I had gotten it right. Maybe that had been his plan all along, or maybe not. But one thing was certain—now that I had said it, it was his plan.

Five of my balls were still on the pool table, and Cedric had only two more to sink. He took aim, then suddenly took a completely different aim, and made the only move that would end the game in a single shot. He put the eight ball in a corner pocket. It was an automatic loss.

"You win," Cedric said. "Guess this wasn't your day to die."

"Dang," said Klutz, who just didn't get it. "I thought you'd win for sure, Cedric."

Cedric laid his cue down on the table. "Time for you to leave, Red."

"What if I don't want to?"

"Not an option."

I took a step closer to him. "Oh, I think it is."

Cedric looked at the others, and then back at me, with a grin. "Are you asking to be a Wolf?"

"Everyone knows what an honor it is to be in your gang," I said.

"Answer the question," said Cedric. "Are you . . . asking . . . to be . . . a Wolf?"

I took a deep breath. "I'm asking to live forever. I'm asking to feel what it's like to be two things at once—man, and animal. I'm asking to be a part of the pack."

"What about your grandma?"

I shrugged. "Her issues aren't mine."

Cedric thought about it and nodded. "Keep it up, Red—you might just get your car back."

I smiled. "I was hoping you might say that." Then I pulled up my sleeve, like I was at the doctor's office getting a shot. "Do it!" I said. "Give me the bite right here, in front of everyone, so they all know I'm one of you."

Cedric put down his cue. "Won't work now," he said. "Only works on the full moon."

I pulled down my sleeve. "Guess I'll just have to wait."

"Fine," Cedric said. "Until then, you'll be a pledge—and if you prove yourself worthy, when the time comes, we'll offer you full membership."

"Fair enough."

"And if I ever think you're not playing straight with me, you're wolfchow."

I nodded. "That's fair, too."

8

PUTTING MARVIN
TO THE TEST

You did *WHAT?*"

If Grandma's hair wasn't already gray, it would have gone that way when I told her that I had confronted Cedric.

"You always said 'keep your friends close, and your enemies closer,'" I reminded her. "Now I'm on the inside."

"I don't know who's more stupid: you, for going to Cedric Soames, or me, for telling you the truth." She wagged a finger at me. "You gotta leave werewolf hunting to the professionals."

"You weren't a professional at first," I reminded her.

Grandma shook her head so hard, I was afraid her teeth might fly out. "I don't want my only grandson to risk getting the bite. No. I forbid it."

"Don't worry, Grandma," I told her. "I know what I'm doing."

She wasn't convinced, and although I wasn't about to admit it, neither was I. See, my performance in the Cave had been the performance of my life, but even then I knew it was only a half lie. As much as I hated the Wolves, there was that restless, impulsive part of me that wanted to know what it was like to change into something fierce: something out of control. Maybe that's what made me so convincing.

"It's brilliant," Marissa said as we sat alone, munching on chips in the antique shop one rainy afternoon. "Scary, but brilliant. Do you think Cedric believes you really want to be a Wolf?"

"I think so."

"Thinking isn't good enough. You have to be sure."

But I knew nothing could be sure. Cedric had no real reason to trust me. Then I thought of something.

"The skull!"

"What about it?"

"Give it to me!"

She looked at me like I was already one of the Wolves. "No."

"Trust me," I said.

She looked at me, not trusting me in the least, then reluctantly she opened a cabinet under the counter. After she looked to make sure no customers were coming in, she pulled out the skull of Xavier Soames and gently set in on the counter. It was a human skull again, but somehow the eye sockets seemed to be watching me. It was smooth and cold to the touch.

I reached for the skull, and Marissa gasped, startling me.

"Marvin's here."

I turned to see him through the shop's glass door, crossing the street toward us, too cool to cover his head from the rain. "Does he know about the skull?"

Marissa shook her head. "If Marvin knew about it, he'd try to show it off—or worse, he'd try to sell it."

I wanted to bring up my concern about Marvin—that he really might be one of the Wolves after all—but I knew mentioning my suspicions would just upset Marissa. She had a blind spot when it came to him.

Marissa hid the skull back beneath the counter as the door opened, setting off the jingle bells above the entrance. Marvin's confident stride broke when he saw me. He picked it up again pretty quickly, though.

"Hi, Marissa," he said, and gave her a brotherly kiss on the cheek. "Hi, Red," he said, with a coolness in his voice he hadn't used when he spoke to her. He looked at me for a moment, then put out his hand like he wanted to shake. I lifted my hand, and he shook it in some strange way that must have been the Wolves' secret handshake.

"Taking an interest in antiques, Red?"

"No, just in your sister," I told him, and winked at her. She threw me back an "oh, please" kind of gaze.

"A lot of guys take an interest," Marvin said. "Few live to tell about it."

Marissa threw him an "oh, please" gaze, too, and Marvin laughed, showing off his gold canine. "Just kidding, Red. Just kidding."

"Ignore him," Marissa said. "He likes to play head games with any boy that comes within five feet of me."

"Hey, that's a big brother's job," I said. "But if he wants to test me, I'll pass any test he wants."

"We'll see," said Marvin.

As it turns out, I wasn't the one to get tested that day.

"Oh," Marissa said, "I just got something in today I want to show you, Red. Something your grandma might like."

Marvin squirmed at the mention of my grandma and turned his attention to the bag of chips we had left on the counter. I didn't quite know what Marissa was up to, only that she was up to something.

She went to a crowded shelf and pulled off a heavy candelabra, reaching for something behind it. Then she held the candelabra out to her brother. "Marvin, could you hold this for a sec?"

Marvin hesitated. At first I didn't realize why he might hesitate. Then it dawned on me. The candelabra was silver.

"Ask Red," Marvin said, leaning casually against the counter, eating chips. "He's closer."

"Hey, man, she asked you," I said.

Marvin sighed and left the chips, stepping over to his sister. I watched to see what would happen. Grandma had said that just touching silver will set off an allergic reaction in a werewolf, whether they were in wolf form or not. It wouldn't be fatal, but it would be painful. If he was a wolf, his hand would turn red and swell up like a balloon in less than a minute. Marissa was putting Marvin to the test.

Marvin gingerly took the candelabra and held it out in front of him like it was a bomb that might detonate at any second.

"I hate holding antiques," he said. "I'm always afraid I'll break them."

Marissa fished around on the shelf a moment more, then came back empty-handed. "That's strange," she said. "I could have sworn it was back here."

Marvin put the candelabra back on the shelf. "Got any dip for those chips?" he said.

Marissa went into the back room, rummaged around a little refrigerator, and came out with a salsa jar that had only dregs left in it. Still, the salsa dregs kept Marvin busy for more than a minute. Long enough for us to see that his hand showed absolutely no reaction from the silver candelabra.

"Listen," he finally said to Marissa. "I came here to drive you home, but if you want to walk in the rain, I got no problem with that."

"Go wait in the car, Marvin," she said. "I've got to close out the register and lock up."

Marvin threw me a suspicious look, then left, letting in the loud patter of rain before the door closed behind him.

Marissa crossed her arms triumphantly. "There. Happy now? That proves he's not a werewolf."

"How come you didn't test *me* like that?" I asked. "Me, you had to hit over the head and tie up."

"Don't be such a baby," she said.

"And anyway, just because he passed the silver test, it still doesn't explain what he's doing hanging around with Cedric."

"Maybe he's just a pledge, like you. Maybe he's pretending, all the while hoping to bring the Wolves down, just like you."

"Or maybe he's pledging for real."

Marissa shook her head. "My brother does *not* want to be a werewolf. He's got something else up his sleeve. I'm sure of it."

I threw up my hands. "Fine, whatever you say. But until we know what *he's* up to, let's not tell him what *we're* up to."

I thought she'd put up an argument, but instead she agreed. Across the street, Marvin honked the horn impatiently.

"You'd better go so I can lock up," Marissa said.

"I still need the skull."

She pulled it out again and handed it to me. I put it in the empty chip bag, which I tucked under my arm.

"When will I get it back?" she asked.

"I don't know. But if you're lucky, you'll end up with a few more for your collection."

It turns out that the Wolves had more than one hangout. They kept themselves mobile so no one would know exactly where they were at any given time. The manager of the Cave was of no help. He didn't know a thing, but I knew someone who would.

As I had predicted, Cedric's sister, Tina, was playing yet another game on the sidewalk of their apartment building. The rain had let up by dusk, and she was out there with a big red ball, bouncing it in puddles, getting her white socks spotted with mud.

"Where's your brother?" I asked her.

"Ain't gonna tell."

"But I'm a friend now."

"You might be a friend, or you might be a fool. So which is it?"

"A little bit of both," I told her.

She looked at the bag in my hands. "That looks too heavy to be a bag of chips," she said. She was way too smart for a seven-year-old. If she ever joined a gang, we were all in for trouble. When I didn't say anything, she bounced her ball up and down, splattering me with puddle water. She bounced it under her leg, then back again, and said in a singsong voice: "Little Red, Little Red, what's in the chip bag, Little Red?"

And in the same singsong voice I answered, "Nothing at all, nothing at all, nothing at all but your grandpa's head."

That made her miss the ball, and it went bouncing across the street, almost getting nailed by a passing car.

"You're not funny," she said. "Now go get my ball."

"Tell me where Cedric is, and I'll get your ball," I told her. "Unless, of course, you want me to tell Cedric you showed disrespect to a Wolf."

She looked at me, a little afraid to tell me, and a little bit afraid not to. "He's in the Troll Bridge Hollow," she said. "Now go get my ball before I tell my mama you been teasing me."

9

▲

TROLL BRIDGE
HOLLOW

Nightshade Boulevard ran into Bleakwood, and Bleakwood ran into Troll. Troll Street went over the river. The Troll Street Bridge was an old gray monster: an iron suspension bridge, with two towers rising like twin tombstones, cables spun like spiderwebs between them. It stretched across the mile-wide river, making you think there was a way out of the city. Like maybe if you crossed it you might find life a little bit easier. But, as everyone knew, when you got to the other side off the Troll Street Bridge, all you found was more of the same.

The bridge itself was the sort of crumbling mess that always seemed minutes away from plunging into the river. Whole chunks of the roadway had fallen away, and you could actually see the river through the potholes. Beneath the roadway, where the bridge touched shore, was a walled-in space at least fifty feet high. In that stone wall beneath the bridge was a single steel door. For as long as I can remember, and before that I'm sure, there were stories about what was behind that door. Some people said there were bodies hidden there, back from the gangster days before even Grandma was born. Others said it was full of gold stolen from Fort Knox. Still others whispered that it held secret stockpiles of nuclear weapons the government had forgotten about.

But the truth was worse than any of that. Troll Bridge Hollow was a werewolf lair.

If there was a secret knock, I didn't know it, so I just pounded on the door until I heard heavy bolts sliding on the other side.

The door creaked open, and in the dim light I saw a pair of eyes, pupils open all the way, like a cat at night.

"Who told you to come here?" It was one of the many Wolves I didn't know.

"I told myself," I said. Although this guy was much bigger than me, I wasn't going to let myself feel threatened. Rule of the jungle: Don't show fear unless you want to be lunch.

"Let him in," I heard Cedric say from somewhere in the darkness of the hollow.

The guy looked at me with a menacing glare.

"You heard him, let me in."

He grunted and stepped aside. I went in and he closed the door behind me. The metallic boom of the closing door echoed in the vast hollow chamber beneath the bridge.

The place had a gamy, damp smell, like wet dog and mildew. It took my eyes a while to adjust, and when they did, I could see that the chamber was full of high brick arches that disappeared into hazy darkness above. I could hear the buzz of traffic on the bridge overhead. The only light came from a TV in the corner, and around it the Wolves stretched out on old couches, watching some bloody action film.

"Our new pledge wants to hang with us," Cedric's voice boomed. He didn't bother to get up from his comfortable couch. "Should we let him?"

"Only if he lets me use him as a footstool," said a kid called A/C, who I guessed was Cedric's second in command. I don't know what his real name was—everyone called him A/C because he always claimed to be "too cool for the room."

Cedric laughed. "You heard him, Red. Go be a footstool."

"Nobody uses me as a footstool."

Cedric's eyes turned from the TV and looked at me, meaner than I thought they could get. "You're a pledge. That means you gotta do whatever we tell you until you're a full-fledged Wolf." Then he grinned a nasty grin. "Or would you rather run crying to your grandma?"

"He knows our hangout," said another voice in the darkness. "If he tells her . . ."

"He won't," said Cedric. "See, we keep a watch on that old witch. If she starts sniffing around here, we'll know Red told her, and that will be the end of Red's story."

I tried not to think about what end Cedric had in mind.

"Do you want to see what I brought you, or not?" I said impatiently.

Finally he got up and stalked toward me. He glanced down at the bag in my hands. "For me? And it ain't even Christmas." A few of the other guys laughed. Not because it was funny, but because Cedric thought it was. Cedric was the kind of guy who had to have his own private laugh track cackling behind his jokes.

"So, what is it?" he asked. "And it better be more than just chips."

I held the bag up to him. "See for yourself."

He took the bag, threw me a suspicious glance, then tried to look inside, but it was too dark. So he reached in, felt around a bit, and his hand came out holding a human skull. He yelped in surprise and dropped it to the musty ground.

"You think that's funny?" Cedric barked.

"Nothing funny about it," I told him. "Take a good look at it. Tell me if it looks familiar, because it should."

By now all the rest of the Wolves had crowded around. Cedric picked up the skull.

"Is it someone I should know?"

"It's your grandpa."

I watched as a whole busload of emotions drove by on Cedric's face. By the time the bus had passed, I could tell he believed me.

"Where did you get this?" he asked through gritted teeth.

Well, I couldn't tell him the truth—but I had a better story anyway, and I knew I could sell it, because lately I'd become a real good liar.

"Where do you think I got it?" I said. "I stole it from my grandma. She had it hanging on the wall like a trophy, in that secret room where she keeps all her werewolf-hunting stuff."

The Wolves all murmured, cursing in awe and anger. Cedric

screwed his lips into a scowl. "That old woman is going down! I won't even wait until the full moon."

"Bad idea," I said. "If you do that, you'll never get all the others."

Cedric looked at me with suspicion written all over his face. "What others?"

"You know . . . The C.W.H."

He gave me a blank look.

"The Confederacy of Werewolf Hunters," I explained. "They're coming into town during the next full moon. They mean to get rid of all of you." And then I corrected myself. "All of *us,* I mean."

The Wolves all looked at one another, whispering worry. Cedric snapped his fingers to shut them up.

"It ain't gonna happen," Cedric said. "Because Red here is going to feed us information and let us know their every move, so we can attack first. Isn't that right, Red?"

"I don't know," I said. "I thought you wanted me to be a footstool."

"You do this right," Cedric said, "and I'll make A/C into *your* footstool."

"Hey!" said A/C.

"Shut up!" said Cedric.

I paused for effect. "Okay, I'll do it," I told him. "On one condition."

"What's the condition?"

"That my grandma doesn't end up in a werewolf's belly."

Cedric looked at me, then broke out laughing. At first I

wasn't sure what his laughter meant. The rest of the Wolves didn't know, either, but they laughed along with him anyway.

"We got ourselves a master negotiator here!" he said.

"Yeah—maybe we oughta send him to negotiate with the Crypts," snorted Loogie. That brought another round of laughter. The Crypts were the all-girl gang whose turf was way across town. Scary bunch, from what I'd heard.

"So," said Cedric, "Little Red's willing to sell out his grandma's life's work in exchange for her life."

"She's a crazy old woman," I told him, "but she's still my grandma, and I want her to live. If you get rid of all her werewolf-hunting friends, you won't have to get rid of her, because she'll be powerless."

Cedric began to pace the big space of the Troll Bridge Hollow, weaving in and out of his pack of Wolves. "Sure," he said. "I'll make her watch all her friends get eaten, and then make her watch as you turn into a werewolf right before her eyes. You're right, Red—letting her live will be a much better revenge. It'll be sweet."

He grinned at A/C, and although A/C grinned back, he looked a little worried—like maybe he really *would* end up being my footstool.

Cedric pointed at me. "You go back to your grandma, but keep your eyes and ears open. Then report back to me."

"I'll be your man on the inside." I turned to go, but Cedric called to me.

"Hey, Red!"

When I turned back to him, something was flying through the air toward me. I snapped my hand up to catch it, and the second it hit my hand, jingling slightly, I knew what it was. My car keys.

"It's parked near the corner of Moat Street and Troll," said Cedric.

I clasped the keys in my hand and felt my heart speed to near breaking. I had my Mustang back! I could have just walked right out of there, gone to my car, and driven off into the sunset, but instead, I threw the keys back to Cedric. "If Grandma sees me with the Mustang, she'll be suspicious. She'll wonder how I got it back. Best if you keep it, and we play enemies for a while."

Cedric smiled. "Red," he said, "I think you might just be too smart for your own good!"

10
▲
"THE WAY OF THE WILD IS OUR WAY, TOO"

I got to know all of the Wolves by name—or at least by the nicknames Cedric had given them. There was Warhead, who was always ready for a fight. There was the kid with a head shaped kind of like an alien's, called Roswell. There was El Toro, Moxie, and the kid named Sherman, who everyone called "the Tank"—twenty-two in all. By the end of my first week, I knew where most of them lived, and they knew where I spent my time, too, because there was always someone tailing me. Cedric wasn't about to trust me entirely—not considering my family tree—so lessons with Grandma on the craft of wolf hunting had to be in short sessions so as to not arouse suspicion.

"Twenty-two Wolves are gonna be hard to put down for a boy, a girl, and an old woman," Grandma said one afternoon. "Especially if we got no master plan."

Grandma was big on "master plans." Me, my plans kind of came to me in spurts. I liked it that way. It kept me on my feet, able to move with the flow of things. But lately that flow was taking some strange new directions.

"It's a dangerous game you're playing, Red," she was always telling me. But at the same time I could see a glimmer of admiration in her eyes. Like tricking Cedric made me worthy of being her grandson.

By the end of the second week, I was the Wolves' official errand boy. They laughed and called me "the Wolverine," like I was a werewolf Cub Scout. I guess they didn't know that a wolverine could be fiercer than a wolf.

All that time I was learning things I couldn't have learned any other way. Like which famous citizens from history had been werewolves (like Frank Sinatra), and how that crazy old woman with the golf-ball eyes managed to get a lock of his hair (you don't want to know).

On the night when the moon had slimmed to a dying crescent in the sky, Cedric took the gang up to the roof of his apartment building, to get away from the heat and humidity that fell on the city like a hot, sopping rag. There was something the others didn't like about going up there. I could tell from the moment Cedric kicked open the door to the roof.

There were a bunch of chairs thrown around up there, still wet from an afternoon rain. In a corner was an old, rusty weight set, and I almost laughed at the thought that werewolves needed to pump iron. Rather than moving into standard hang poses, the Wolves just waited at the door. Loogie coughed up a wad and spat it, hitting Klutz's shoe. They fought about it until Cedric shouted at them, and they stopped.

I didn't like this. I didn't like the way they were all acting, like they were scared of something up here. Just then Cedric came up behind me and kicked me to the ground.

"Ow!" I scraped my arm on the gritty tar paper of the roof.

"The Wolverine's gotta toughen himself up," Cedric said. I tried to get up, and he put a foot on my chest, pushing me down again.

"You want my help, stop treating me like an animal."

"We're the animals," he said. "But you haven't earned your fangs yet."

I got up and readied myself for the next blow. "So I gotta let you beat me up? That's how I earn my fangs?"

A/C came forward. "The pack leader's gotta show his dominance," he said. "The way of the wild is our way, too."

"He fought us all up here," said Marvin, smiling like he couldn't wait to see me beaten to a pulp.

Cedric spun and did a roundhouse kick, smashing me in the side of the head. It would have been more lethal if he actually knew karate, but even so, it was pretty painful. It knocked me to my knees, but I got right back up. He tried it again, but this time I caught his leg and pushed him back.

The other Wolves backed away. The Wolf everyone called El Toro came up to me and whispered, "Don't fight back. Just take it."

Sorry, but that just wasn't the way I was made.

Cedric lunged at me. I stepped aside and threw my fist into his gut. It hurt him, because he wasn't ready, but he tried not to show it. He punched me in the stomach twice as hard, then grabbed me before I could double over from the pain. He lifted me off the ground, and before I knew it, I couldn't see ground beneath me at all—just air. He was holding me by the front of my shirt out over the edge of the fifteen-story roof. I couldn't see his eyes in the dim rooftop light, but I could hear his fury. It came in snarling breaths.

"You hit me!" he growled. "After all I've done for you, you hit me!"

"Self-defense," I said. I tried to squirm out of his grip, and then I realized how stupid that would be—if he lost his grip, I'd fall to my death. The panic was welling up inside of me like a bad school lunch. I tried to speak again, but only a pitiful squeak came out.

"Cedric, don't!" yelled A/C. "He's not a Wolf yet! He'll die!"

A sneaker slipped from my foot, but I never heard it hit the ground, because the ground was so far away. I could still hear the wild snarl in Cedric's voice. "Do you know what happens when one of us falls from this roof?"

"What?" I squeaked out, figuring that if he keeps talking, he's not dropping.

"I knocked Loogie off a few weeks ago," Cedric said. "Accident."

Yeah, right, I thought. *Like Hiroshima was an accident.* It seemed to me Cedric liked to use Loogie for experiments, like seeing what would happen if a werewolf fell off a roof.

"He landed flat on his back, got broken up real bad."

"Yeah," said Klutz. "It turned him into a sidewalk Loogie."

That started Klutz and Loogie fighting again.

"It sure did hurt, but he healed in a few days," Cedric said. "Werewolves do. But you won't."

"Drop me, and you lose your edge on the hunters," I told him.

"Beg," he demanded. "Beg me not to kill you."

I flashed to the time he had choked me, and I gave up Grandma's money to save myself. Money's one thing, but self-respect is another. I don't beg. Not even for my life. So I whispered so only Cedric could hear, "I think you showed enough dominance."

I thought he'd either drop me or throw me back onto the roof. Instead, he set me gently back on my feet. His rage had passed like a summer thunderhead, all rained out before you could find an umbrella.

"Good for you, Wolverine," he said. "You're one step closer."

"He didn't bleed! He didn't bruise!" Marvin complained. "Not even a black eye!"

"You got a problem?" yelled Cedric. "Maybe you want to take a flying leap today?"

That shut Marvin up. The other Wolves came up around me, to congratulate me for passing Cedric's test—I guess the only rule for passing is that you survive. They patted me on the back, they gave me the secret handshake. It took the edge off the anger I felt toward Cedric. In fact, in spite of what I had just been through, I felt an odd sense of accomplishment. A sense of pride.

But I'm just pretending to be one of them, aren't I? Aren't I?

Still, I didn't tell Grandma or Marissa about what happened on that roof.

I didn't see much of Marissa during my first two weeks as a Wolf pledge because Cedric kept me so busy. I went to the antique shop when I could, but the owner was there most of the time, or there were customers, so Marissa and I couldn't really talk. We did get to sit and eat hot dogs one evening on the end of a pier. We had to meet there because it was the only place I knew I could go where a spying Wolf couldn't get close enough to listen.

"Your grandma is teaching me all the stuff you're not getting to learn," Marissa told me. She took another bite of her dog and spoke with her mouth full. I can respect a girl who talks with her mouth full. "Even if you don't know something, I will, so by the time the moon gets full again, we'll be ready."

"Like what stuff is she teaching you?" I was a bit jealous that she got to spend more time with Grandma than me.

"You know," she said, like it was nothing. "How to track supernatural beasts with an ectoplasmic lens, how to slow their transformations with eye of newt and baking soda. Those kinds of things."

"Oh."

"Tell me everything *you've* learned!" Marissa said. But I shook my head. "Nothing important. Nothing we'll need." She now knew ancient secrets from mysterious werewolf hunters of the past. So I would have some secrets, too.

"Enough of that," I said. "Let's talk about something else."

"What else is there to talk about?"

"Anything but werewolves," I said. And so we talked about the upcoming year at school, movies we wanted to see, music that made you want to dance, and anything that came to mind.

Spending time with Marissa, even though it was only half an hour or so, made everything feel normal just for a while. The fresh river air seemed to blow away all thoughts of dark and unnatural things. But when we left the pier, she went one way, I went another, and there I was again, in the shadows of buildings, facing the hard concrete reality of Wolves that hid within human flesh.

Tonight would be the new moon, the darkest night of July. Only the stars would peer down from the sky above, so hard to see in the city. It was less than two weeks until the moon would be full again, but I was wasting my time with Marissa, talking about silly things instead of plotting werewolf doom.

I took a shortcut, leaving the relative safety of the busy streets, and turned down an alley full of Dumpsters and deep shadows. It was the kind of place where you find police chalk outlines in the morning. It wasn't too smart of me to walk down that way, but I've always been a little too bold for my own good. My mom would call it foolhardy. Grandma would call it just plain dumb.

Maybe it was just that I felt kind of safe now, being a pledge to the Wolves. Lately, when I got the feeling I was being stalked, I knew it was one of them, tailing me on Cedric's orders. Oddly enough, it gave me a feeling of security, because I was in with them now, and if some thugs ever did actually jump me, I had the distinct feeling that one of my Wolf brothers would be right there to help me fight them off.

Wolf brothers.

It kind of tweaked my spine to think of them as brothers . . . but then, being a brother didn't always mean that you meant one another well. My mom, who was an all-occasion Bible quoter, often told of poor Abel, who was killed by his brother Cain in a field. So if the Wolves were my brothers now, did that make me Cain or Abel? I knew I shouldn't think too much on it, but lately I couldn't help it.

With so much on my mind, I wasn't as observant as I should have been. I was ambushed halfway down the alley. My attacker fell on me, big and broad, cutting across my vision like the moon eclipsing the sun. He smashed into me, and I bounced against a big green Dumpster, my head making the metal ring like I was a bell clapper. I turned and swung, but I was so disoriented, I caught nothing but air. The momentum of my own punch spun me around, I slipped in a puddle of alley scum, and hit the ground. When I looked up, I saw that it was none other than Marvin Flowers.

My brain was still too scrambled to speak, but that was just fine with Marvin.

"There's something you had better get straight," he growled. "You wanna be a Wolf, I got no problem with that. But you stay away from my sister." There was a fury in his eyes, and it was nothing like the fury of a wolf. It was human through and through, but that didn't make it any less dangerous.

I could have fought with him, but it wouldn't have been too wise. I was a head shorter, he was still beefed up from his years of football, and his fury gave him even more of an advantage. No, it was unlikely that I'd win this fight with muscle, but maybe I could put a dent in him with words, before he dented the Dumpster with me.

"What's the matter, Marvin? Wolves aren't good enough for

your sister? Maybe I should tell Cedric, and see what he thinks?" That gave him pause for thought. With my back against the Dumpster, I pushed myself back to my feet. "How long have you been waiting to get made, Marvin?" I asked. "How many months? Cedric must not be too happy with you if he's waited this long."

The anger didn't leave Marvin's face, but his eyebrows knotted with something between confusion and disgust. "What are your lips flapping about?"

"You might act like a werewolf, but you're not one! I saw you touch that silver candleholder. If you were a real werewolf, just touching it would make you swell up like one of those balloons in the Thanksgiving Day parade. You're just a pledge like me, and you're mad because you think I'll get 'made' before you do."

"You don't know what you're talking about," he grumbled, but I could tell I had my thumb on a nerve now. "You think you know things," Marvin said, "but you know absolutely nothing."

"You forget that my grandma's a werewolf hunter, and taught me all there is to know about it. So you could say I knew exactly what I was getting into when I decided to join the Wolves. Probably more than anyone else who's ever joined."

Marvin was quiet. I knew I was getting to him. "So tell me, how come Marvelous Marvin Flowers hasn't gotten the bite yet?"

Then Marvin's blank expression stretched into a smile, which was never a good thing. "Maybe Cedric wants it that way," he said. "Maybe Cedric needs a human lookout on the nights they go wolfing."

Well, it made sense, but there was something beneath Marvin's gold-toothed grin that was as slimy as a morning snail trail. It made everything he said suspect.

"So, are you gonna stay away from my sister, or not?"

"You were the one who sent me in her direction when you went to steal my grandma's money."

"That was then," he said. "This is now."

A truck turned down the alley. I suppose the sight of other activity in the alley made me feel a little bit bolder. "I make no promises as far as your sister is concerned."

Marvin pursed his lips and nodded. "We could have been friends, Red. But it looks like you just made yourself an enemy." And with that, he grabbed me, lifted me off the ground, and hurled me with his beefy, varsity-trained arms into the Dumpster.

I landed in the trash headfirst, and it was the worst kind of garbage. Rotten vegetables, greasy pasta dregs, and other awful restaurant trash. I righted myself, which was hard in the slippery grunge, and suddenly felt something brush across my leg. A pink tail slithered past, attached to a nasty-looking rat. I scrambled to get away, but it didn't matter. Rats were everywhere.

"Marvin!" This was one of those high Dumpsters, and climbing out wasn't going to be easy. A rat eyed me with dead-eyed suspicion. "Marvin, I'm gonna kill you, you creep!"

The groan of the truck engine grew louder. Hopefully whoever was in that truck had seen Marvin throw me in and would help me out. I tried to work my way to the side of the Dumpster, but it was slow moving, and I kept slipping on the maggoty garbage. There was the sudden clang of metal against metal, followed by another clang, and the whole Dumpster shifted. The rats scrambled up the sides and escaped in a way I could not. That's when I realized what was going on—and what Marvin had intended when he tossed me in here.

The truck that had turned down the alley was a trash truck.

The Dumpster began to rise and the floor to tilt, garbage pouring all over me. My feet slid out from under me on the slippery rot. "Hey," I screamed, "stop!" But who was I kidding? No one could hear me over the drone of the trash truck. As the Dumpster tilted, I saw that the garbage wasn't just food crud. There were planks of wood, broken bricks, and iron rods from some nearby construction. In a few seconds it was all going to be on top of me, and I thought, *What a stupid way to die, tossed out with the trash.* I pulled my knees to my chest, gripping my head in crash position, like they do on doomed airplanes, and I said prayers I thought I had forgotten as the whole Dumpster was flipped upside down. I fell into the truck. Iron rods came down on me, missing most of my body, but scraping up my arms real bad. A brick nailed me on the forehead in spite of every attempt to shield my face.

When the trash had settled, and the Dumpster was banging its way back down to the ground, I ran a system check on my whole body. Once I was sure I wasn't dead, I struggled out from underneath the garbage. The trash truck was almost full. I never thought being in a full trash truck could ever be a good thing. But all that garbage beneath me allowed me to get a good grip on the truck's edge and pull myself up. The truck had already left the alley, and with my arm slung over the edge,

I waited, hoping that the driver didn't get the bright idea of turning on the compactor while I was hanging there.

We stopped at a red light, and I leaped out, falling to the road. It must have been quite a sight to the other drivers, but that was the last thing I cared about right then. At a nearby corner I snagged some ice from a street vendor's soda bin and pressed it to the knot on my forehead.

So Marvin wanted a war. That was fine by me, because I was more than ready to fight one.

11
THE CANYONS

My mom must have known I was into something over my head. I could tell by the way she looked at me, and the way she judged my answers to innocent questions, as if there was hidden meaning in everything I said. I think my parents would have canceled their vacation if it hadn't already been paid for. They were taking a two-week cruise on the Mediterranean. Their second honeymoon. It was fine by me, because I didn't have to go skulking around anymore and make up stories about where I had been. And besides, I was getting more and more restless. I couldn't imagine being confined on something as small as a ship.

Right before they left, Mom did something strange.

"I want to give you something, Red."

I followed her into her room, and she went to a secret compartment in her jewelry chest and pulled out a little coin on a chain. She pointed to the face on the front. "This is Saint Gabriel," she said. "Saint Gabriel of the Sorrowful Mother. He's a patron saint of young people."

The coin was silver and looked very, very old. At first I hesitated, almost afraid to touch it, as if the silver might . . . I shook off the feeling. I had no problem with silver. None at all. I took the coin from her and rubbed it between my fingers, just to prove it to myself.

"Your grandmother gave this to me when I was about your age. It was the day before your grandpa died."

My eyes snapped up to her. I could tell by looking at her that she didn't know the truth about how he died, any more than I did—although I did have my suspicions.

"I want you to have it," my mom said. "Wear it while we're gone, so Saint Gabriel will protect you."

"Sure, Mom," I said. "Sure, I'll wear it." I almost told her everything right then. I wanted to tell her about the Wolves, and how I was supposed to hate them, but when you spend your days with evil, some of it is bound to soak into your clothes, like cigar smoke in a closed room. I wanted to explain to her, but how could I when I couldn't even explain it to myself? In the end, all I said was, "Thanks."

Mom looked at me, studying me for all the layers of meaning beneath my one-word answer, then finally gave up with a sigh.

"Close to your heart," she said, so I slipped the medallion over my neck and tucked it beneath my shirt. It wasn't exactly a werewolf hunter's medallion, but at least it would remind me which side I was supposed to be on.

It turns out Mom wasn't the only one who had something for me. When I arrived at Troll Bridge Hollow later that afternoon, Cedric had a new task for his errand boy. He gave me a sealed envelope with an address scrawled on it.

"I need you to deliver this for me," he said. "Go straight there, now."

"What is it?"

"That's not your business!" he barked. "Your business is just to deliver it. Mess up, and I mess *you* up."

I left dutifully, as I always did, to run my errand for the Wolves.

The address was clear across town, way out of the Wolves' turf, a place everyone called "the Canyons." It was a bleak corner of the world where I had never been, and had never cared to go. They called it the Canyons because it was full of huge abandoned warehouses looming over narrow streets where not even crabgrass dared to grow in the cracked sidewalks. The streets were canyons of shadow: dark crevasses that rarely let in the sun.

I crossed through Abject End Park, an overgrown no-man's-land that divided our part of town from the Canyons, then crossed over into that awful, dead place. Street after street of dead factories with broken, soulless windows looked out over burned-out cars, which leaned like shipwrecks on the curb.

I rechecked the address on the envelope and counted the building numbers past a forgotten linen factory to a little church on a corner, which seemed completely out of place. The church's paint had peeled down to the warping wood grain, and like everything else in the Canyons, it looked like no one had been here for years. My mama didn't like dead churches. "There's nothing more unholy than abandoned holy ground," she once said.

Sending me here was a joke, of course—it had to be. I could just imagine Cedric laughing his head off about it. I knocked on the door, counted to three, and turned to leave, already plotting the most direct path out of the godforsaken canyons. Then, as I crossed the street, I heard the sound of creaking hinges. I turned to see a figure in black standing just inside the open door. My heart missed a beat.

"Are you a Wolf?" said a girl's voice.

"Uh . . . yeah," I said.

"She says you can come in."

She, I thought. *She, who?*

The girl at the door was about as inviting as the Grim Reaper on Good Friday, so I wasn't in a hurry to hang with her or any of her Goth friends. I took my time crossing back to the church, hoping I could put together enough of the loose pieces of this situation to figure out what this was all about.

Wait . . . I thought. *Goth girls in a ruined church? Could Cedric have sent me on an errand to the Wolves' only rival gang in town?*

I reached the door, but didn't really feel like crossing the threshold, so I just held out the envelope. "Here."

The girl stood in shadows so dim, I couldn't see much of her face. She didn't reach for the envelope.

"Didn't you hear me? She said you can come in."

"What if I don't feel like it?"

"She doesn't care what you feel like."

There was no doubt in my mind now. I knew who they were. "Are you . . . the *Crypts?*"

"If you have to ask, then you don't deserve an answer," she

said. I wish Cedric had warned me that he was sending me down the throat of a rival gang.

"Her patience grows thin," said the ghoulie-girl in the shadows.

Against my better judgment I went in. Seems this summer was just full of things that were against my better judgment. The inside of the church was as bleak as the outside, filled with crumbling pews beneath windows covered in layer after layer of boards. A few stray votive candles cast the only light in the dreary space, and the place was even mustier than Troll Bridge Hollow, if that was possible. The door closed behind me. The creepy girl who had let me in must have slunk away into some dark corner—and in this place every corner was dark.

There was a smell beyond the waxy scent of the candles—something unpleasant that I couldn't name—but whatever it was, it made my neck hairs stand on end. At the front of the church, where the pulpit once stood, was another girl in black, but her dress was nothing like the wrinkled cotton the girl at the door wore. It was the kind of silky, slinky dress you might wear to a fancy ball, but I don't think she was going anywhere. She stood there in the spot like she owned the place. Not just the place, but the Canyons themselves—and being the leader of the Crypts, I guess she did. I approached her.

"Cedric sent you," she said, more a statement than a question. "I've been waiting for you." Her voice was both powerful and musical. Commanding, yet soothing. It was the type of voice that could lull you to sleep. Just listening to her made my defenses relax, like some strange reflex deep down inside me.

"Yeah, I got a letter for you," I said. As I got closer I could see the strange accessories of her outfit. Odd white earrings dangled like icicles from her lobes. A black, spiked bracelet was wrapped around each of her wrists. She was African-American, and yet oddly pale at the same time. Her skin didn't have that healthy chocolate tone that my grandfather's had had. Instead, her skin was almost purple: the color of a bruise. I handed the envelope to her. She took it with her long fingers. Her nails were painted the same color as her skin, looking like roaches on the end of her fingers. Rather than opening the envelope, she took a long look at me and said in that deep musical voice. "You're not a true Wolf. I can smell it; you reek of mortality."

"That's not your business," I told her. "That's between me and Cedric."

"Fair enough." Using a fingernail as a letter opener, she sliced the side of the envelope and pulled out a note. I watched her eyes as they darted back and forth across the page. I sensed intelligence there.

"Where are the rest of the Crypts?" I asked. "Or is the whole gang just you and the girl at the door?"

The look on her face darkened. "If you're trying to count how many of us there are, to report back to the Wolves, you won't be able to—but believe me, there are many more of us than there are in your little pack."

I put up my hands apologetically. "Didn't mean to rub you the wrong way. Just curious."

She took a moment to judge me honestly and said, "The Crypts are all here. You're just not looking in the right places."

She finished reading the note. Her dangling earrings rattled with every movement of her head, and only now did I realize what they were. Human finger bones.

When she was done with the letter, she turned her eyes from the paper to me again, studying me as intensely as she had studied the letter. "What's your name?"

"Everyone just calls me Red."

She grinned. "Are you the Red Rider?"

I have to admit I was impressed. I didn't know I had a reputation. "Yeah, that's me. So how come you know me?"

"You don't remember me, do you?" she said. Again, a statement more than a question. I found it hard to believe that I could forget someone like this, but I drew a total blank. She smiled even wider. It was almost warm. "I used to be your babysitter. In the days before."

All at once it came to me—not a memory of her face, but a memory of her style. The way her hands would move across a game board. The way she would sing to me when I went to sleep. For an instant I flashed on a memory of her perfume—sort of vanilla and spice. She didn't smell like that now, though. She had the same strange, unnamable smell as the rest of this place.

"Rowena?"

"So you do remember me!"

I nodded. I couldn't imagine my parents trusting me to the hands of a babysitter like this. . . . But I guess she wasn't always like this.

"You were a sweet kid," she said.

I frowned and pushed up my shoulders. "Yeah, well, sweet doesn't get you much in this town."

"It can get you further than you think," she said.

"Were you always so mysterious? I don't remember that."

She responded with a silence as mysterious as her words. Pulling a pen out of thin air, it seemed, she flipped over the note and scribbled on the back of it. "Take this back to Cedric," she said, handing it back to me.

She took no care to conceal the note in an envelope, or even to fold it so that I couldn't read it. Somehow I sensed she wanted me to read it, so I did. The message read:

IT IS AGREED.

SEND HIM AT MIDNIGHT,

THREE NIGHTS IN A ROW.

"You can go now," she said.

"Can I ask what the message means?"

"Better if you don't."

Knowing I'd get no more out of her, I turned to go, and as I neared the door, the first girl appeared out of the shadows, opening it for me.

"A word to the wise, Red," Rowena called out from behind me. "If you can't stay on Cedric's good side, then stay out of his way entirely."

Then the door slammed closed behind me, and I was alone in the stark shadows of the dead industrial canyons.

12

A FEW MILLION WEREWOLVES

Being a double agent takes a toll on you. You spend your days lying, pretending to accept friendship like you mean it, knowing you're going to betray those same people who trust you. Cedric had so much power in his gang, but in a way I had even more power than him. Their fate rested entirely on me. I could save them by telling the truth. I could destroy them by lying. No one should have that much power.

When a growing half-moon hung above the city, Cedric took us all back to the roof of his apartment building, to give me the big talk. It was a week until the night of first change.

"You want to know why there are werewolves?" Cedric asked as we sat in rusty chairs on the roof. It wasn't as dark as it had been that first time, and I found myself less terrified than I had been then. The memory of being held out over fifteen stories of thin air isn't something that fades too quickly. Somehow I couldn't help but think this was another test.

"There are werewolves because one of your ancestors got bit by one," I told him.

"That's not what I mean." He pushed himself closer, the legs of his chair scraping on the gritty tar paper of the roof. The rest of the Wolves sat in a circle around us, like this was another secret rite of the werewolf order.

"Everything on Earth is here for a reason," Cedric said. "Trees are here to make oxygen, worms are here to make dirt. There's no such thing as a freak of nature. If it's here, it's naturally meant to be here."

Unnaturally, in your case. I didn't dare say it out loud.

"Most other animals got predators to keep their population down—but see, us humans are too smart for predators. Even the stupid humans like Klutz."

The others razzed Klutz, and he threw a few well-placed punches to shut them up.

"We build walls and fences to keep the predators out," Cedric said. "We put 'em in zoos, and the ones that get loose, we can put 'em down with a single rifle shot. See, we got brains."

"So, what's your point?"

"I'm getting to that." Cedric leaned forward. "It used to be that diseases kept the human population in control. Before we knew how to fight them, things like the plague came and wiped out people like flies—but not anymore. We got vaccines, and antibiotics, and Pepto-Bismol and stuff, so suddenly the bugs ain't so bad anymore." He looked around to make sure he had everyone's attention, although I got the feeling they'd all heard this a dozen times before—every time a new Wolf was going to be "made."

Cedric spread out his arms. "So here I am, Mother Nature, trying to figure out how to keep humans down, on account of the population is reaching like a gazillion."

"Six billion," I told him.

"Whatever. Anyway, Mother Nature scratches her head, thinks for a while, and says, 'Hey, I know—I'll come up with a predator as smart as a human. One with a thirst for human blood.' She can't use evolution, though, because that takes too long, and she don't got that much patience. She needs to work herself up something real quick . . . so what do you think she does?"

I wanted to answer with something obnoxious, like "She goes on eBay," but the truth was, I couldn't answer him. All I could do was listen, my mouth dry, my throat closed up, and my eyes fixed on those yellow eyes in front of me.

"Mother Nature," Cedric proclaimed proudly, "creates werewolves to solve the problem. Oh, she'd been working on us for a thousand years or so, and with each generation we've gotten stronger. Hungrier."

Cedric's logic was as twisted as his supernatural DNA. I found myself amazed by how he stretched everything to fit the way he saw the world. A person could fall into that, believing the things he said.

"In ten years, how many more gazillions of people will be on this world if something's not done about it?" he said. "A few million werewolves could take care of the problem just like that," and he snapped his fingers, like he could magically create a few million werewolves. Then I realized that he could. Bite enough people, who then bite more people, and pretty soon, werewolf'll be the world's fastest-growing ethnic group.

"Of course it will take time," Cedric said. "But we're ready to start expanding outward. Next month A/C is heading out to Chicago to start his own pack there. Warhead will be going to Los Angeles. I figure in less than a year we'll have packs in twenty cities."

The air on the rooftop suddenly felt thin, like I was trying to breathe in space. I thought I might pass out, then I realized I'd been hyperventilating, breathing in and out so fast I was getting dizzy. I couldn't tell if it was excitement, or fear.

"And we won't be just your ordinary werewolves. No! See, I've got another trick up my sleeve. One that I don't even think Mother Nature was counting on."

"He still won't even tell *us* what it is," grumbled A/C.

"*I* know what it is," Loogie said, but Cedric threw him a silencing gaze.

"Why are you telling me all this?" I said, trying to slow my breathing.

"You're one of us now," said Klutz, looking to Cedric for approval.

"Right," Cedric said. "You deserve to know what's in your future."

I looked around and saw that one of the Wolves was hanging back. "How about you, Marvin?" I said. "What city are you going to?"

"None of your business," Marvin snapped.

"You gotta be with us for a year before you can start your own pack in a new city," Cedric told me. Then he smiled. "But that doesn't mean you can't make your reservation now." He snapped his fingers, and then Warhead stood up, taking a map out of his pocket, unfolding it on an air duct beside us. It was a map of the United States. More than twenty cities were marked off, claimed by each of the Wolves. I could sense a hint of the werewolf coming to the surface in Cedric. Whether it was a hunger for flesh, or a hunger for power, I didn't know.

"Pick yourself a city," he said.

I looked at him, and at A/C and Klutz. I looked at Warhead and Marvin. I stood, and feeling lighter than air, I went over to the map. Klutz handed me a marker. The permanent kind.

"Go on," Cedric said. "Any city that's not already taken."

I looked at the map, holding the marker in my hand. Any city I want. Grandma was right. This was a dangerous game.

"Denver," I said. "I want Denver." And I marked the city with an *X,* claiming it in my name.

The next day I told Grandma that Cedric had big plans, but I didn't tell her what those plans were. I figured she didn't really need to know, since it really didn't change anything as far as she was concerned. Her goal . . . our goal . . . was to take out every single werewolf, and Cedric's plan didn't change that. "He's smart," I told Grandma. "A lot smarter than you give him credit for."

That was something Grandma did not want to hear. It upset

her so bad, she burned the eggs she was cooking. That might not sound like much, but Grandma was the coolest customer I knew. Nothing ever seemed to rattle her. Even when the Wolves had locked us in her basement, she was calm.

"I was so sure he'd be like his grandfather," she said. "Xavier Soames was shortsighted and simpleminded. A werewolf with brains is a frightening foe."

"Grandma," I asked, "you never did tell me how you got Xavier."

Grandma cleaned out the burned pan.

"I didn't get him," she said. "Your grandfather did." At first I thought she wasn't going to tell me any more, but she put the pan down and turned off the faucet. Her glasses were steamed up from the hot water, and when she took them off, I could see her eyes were a little moist, too. She sat down at the kitchen table, and I sat with her. "We had gotten the rest of the gang, but we knew if we didn't get Xavier, he'd be able to gather a whole new pack, and so we couldn't wait. Your grandpa knew Xavier was going to be harder, more dangerous, than the rest. He was the strongest, the fastest, the most brutal of all of them. Your grandpa didn't want me to risk it, so on the next full moon, he snuck out alone, without telling me, to track Xavier down. Xavier had been hiding out for a month down by the docks. Your grandfather found him in an old, burned-out warehouse. He hoped to surprise him, catching him before the moon rose, but it didn't happen that way. By the time he found Xavier, he was already in wolf form, and hungry. Just before Xavier pounced, your grandfather raised his gun and pulled the trigger.

His aim was true, and the bullet sank deep in the werewolf's chest. It stunned him, but only for a moment—and even though your grandfather had filled up on wolfsbane tea, when a werewolf as powerful as Xavier is furious enough, it won't make a bit of difference."

I was at the edge of my seat now. Grandma took a moment to blow her nose and wipe her eyes. This was hard on her, and I thought I knew what was coming next. I had always heard that Grandpa had died of blood poisoning. But was I about to find out he was really killed by a werewolf? Suddenly I didn't want to hear any more, but I couldn't stop listening.

"Your grandfather ran, Red. He had a plan, you see. He raced to his Harley, then took off, with Xavier right on his tail. Xavier must have known he had less than a minute to live before the silver of the bullet took effect, and he was determined to take your grandfather with him. They were just at the edge of the river, and your grandfather blasted full-throttle down Pier Twenty-four, and soared off the end right into the ice-cold winter water. When he surfaced and looked back, he could see Xavier still there on the edge of the pier writhing in pain, his cells exploding from the inside out. From that icy water your grandfather watched Xavier die. It wasn't until he got home and told me the whole story that he noticed a small cut on his heel. Xavier had nipped at his heel just before he rode into the water. It was barely a scratch, but sometimes all it takes is a little bite.

"All the next day we sat together, waiting. If that tiny bite from Xavier had passed on the curse, we would know when the moon rose that night. At about four that afternoon, he went into the darkroom. 'I just want to make a few quick prints,' he said. 'To pass the time.' He was in there for more than an hour, and I began to get worried." Grandma paused. I suppose she had never told this to anyone. "I found him on the floor of the darkroom, with a small piece of paper in his mouth."

Grandma didn't have to say another word. I knew exactly what had happened.

"Silver bromide!" I said. Grandma had taught me enough about photography over the years for me know about silver bromide—the stuff on photographic paper that makes it work. "It was a piece of photographic paper in his mouth, wasn't it, Grandma?"

Grandma nodded, scrunching her face up to try to hold back the tears. "To someone with the werewolf curse, the stuff's like cyanide. He left a note. He said this was a better test than waiting to see what happened when the moon rose. Because if he was a werewolf, he didn't want to live long enough to actually become one."

Grandma cried, and I reached out to hold her hand. So in a way, it had been blood poisoning after all.

"I'm sorry," I said.

Grandma quickly mopped up her tears. "It was a long time ago. But if his sacrifice is going to mean anything, we have to finish the job. We have to get rid of Cedric Soames and his new gang, and make sure not a single one of them survives this full moon." Then she took a good look at me. "Is there anything else you found out about them? Anything that can help us?"

"Nothing else."

"You sure?"

"Of course I'm sure."

"All right, then."

I didn't tell her that Cedric had offered me a city—or that part of me had liked the idea.

None of the Wolves questioned my loyalty anymore. They didn't look at me funny, didn't doubt my motives. Except, of course, for Marvin, who just got more and more bitter with every ounce of acceptance I got. I had respect down there in the Troll Bridge Hollow now, and it made me feel powerful. It was the kind of sneaky, addictive power that kept making you want more. I wasn't exactly sure why I had so much respect now. Maybe it was because I knew so much about "the Confederation of Werewolf Hunters," which didn't even exist. I even made up names for some of them. I got them off the spines of books on my grandma's shelf and mixed them up. "Herman King." "Stephen Melville." Or maybe they respected me because I had ventured into the Canyons and had actually set foot in the Crypts' lair. Of course, the Wolves wouldn't admit that they were afraid of the Crypts.

"They're just a bunch of girls," Klutz had said over a game of pool in the Cave one day. Some of the Wolves grunted in agreement.

"Just a bunch of girls, huh?" Cedric smacked him in the head. "You're even dumber than you look. Girls can be just as tough as guys when they wanna be. Sometimes even tougher." He took away Klutz's cue and made a shot for him, even though Cedric wasn't in the game. "All I know is I wouldn't want another war with the Crypts—and I ain't ashamed to admit that either." Then he gave Klutz a twisted grin. "Of course, if you want to take them on by yourself, be my guest—and see if you don't end up like Bobby Tanaka."

"Who's Bobby Tanaka?" I asked.

"You mean who . . . *was* Bobby Tanaka."

A/C chuckled nervously. "Yeah," he explained, "he was a Wolf, but the Crypts kinda put him in past tense."

"Got him with silver?" I asked.

Cedric shook his head. "No."

"But I thought *'silverizing'* was the only way to kill a werewolf."

"It is," Cedric said. "But some things are worse than death."

It seemed to me the temperature in the room dropped, and the Wolves let out a collective shiver.

Klutz began to look a little pale, like all his macho was leaking out through the holes in his Nikes.

"We don't talk much about Bobby anymore," Cedric said. "Or the Crypts. They stay on their side of town; we stay on ours. Everybody's happy."

"So why did I get sent over there?" I dared to ask. "And who did she want you to send for three midnights in a row?"

I thought Cedric might whack me in the head, too, but he didn't. He just gave Klutz his cue stick back and took Loogie's soda, like it was his own. It was an unspoken rule: Whatever was yours was also Cedric's. Which maybe explained why none of the Wolves ever showed up with their girlfriends.

"You're full of questions today, Little Red."

But Cedric offered me no answers. Instead, he demanded to know more about the so-called Confederacy of Werewolf

Hunters, so I made up stories about John Steel and Danielle Grisham, and how they were, at this very minute, flying in from London.

As for Grandma, she thought the stories I was feeding the Wolves were a fine thing. "When you're at war, like we are, it's not called 'lies,' it's called *disinformation,*" Grandma said. "Spreading disinformation is a powerful weapon. If they think they're outmatched and outnumbered, they'll be scared and start doing stupid things. That's when we'll have them!"

I couldn't tell her how spinning all those lies to Cedric was making me feel all twisted up inside.

I had once told Cedric that Grandma had a secret room where she kept all her werewolf stuff. Good thing he never came back to look for himself because there was no such place. There was a darkroom, but that hadn't been used for years. All that was in there were old photographic supplies. Grandma's werewolf work was done out in the open; the only thing shielding it from prying eyes were her venetian blinds.

Four days before the first full moon, she was working a blowtorch, melting down silver jewelry into bullet slugs on the same table where she served Thanksgiving dinner.

"Silver bullets aren't exactly an item you get at Wal-Mart," she told me. "You gotta make them yourself, but you have to be careful."

I watched her pour the molten silver into little molds, like she was making a pie. She had bought a whole bunch of .22-caliber shells and had removed the bullets, replacing them with the silver ones once they had cooled in the mold. "Not exactly rocket science," she said, "but if you do a shoddy job, the bullet may just blow up in the barrel—or in your hand."

"I hate guns," I mumbled to myself, but Grandma heard.

"Don't you worry, Red—I got you covered," she said. She took off her protective glasses and went into the closet, coming out with something you don't usually find in your grandma's closet. It was a steel crossbow.

"Ever use one of these?"

"No," I said. I had spent a couple of weeks in summer camp once and did some archery there, but this wasn't summer-camp archery we were talking about.

"I'm making you some silver-tipped arrows. They'll do the job."

I took it from her and held it by its smooth ivory handle. It was heavy, but so well balanced, it felt half its weight. A cross-bow was different from a gun. Crossbows were always in the hands of good guys. At least in the movies. I found that I could stand to hold it, in a way I could never stand to hold a gun. This was a fine anti-werewolf weapon.

"A werewolf's a big target, but it'll also be moving," she said. "You're going to need practice."

13

▲

ABJECT END PARK

Crossbow practice needs space. Crossbow practice needs solitude. And, most importantly, crossbow practice requires a target—in my case, a very *big* target—and one that can stop an arrow without splintering it. Like the massively thick oaks that have taken over Abject End Park—the border between our part of town and the ruined buildings of the Canyons.

I figured the best time to practice would be at dawn. Aside from the occasional cop car or garbage truck, the city would still be asleep—and so would the Wolves, sleeping off whatever mayhem they had gotten into the night before. As long as I got back home before any of them were up and about, they wouldn't know what I was doing.

I set my alarm for 4:30 A.M. and was in the park just as the sun was beginning to rise, turning the eastern sky a grimy yellow. It was barely sunrise, and the day was already beginning to get hot.

Marissa was already there, waiting for me. "So you made it."

She stifled a yawn as she stepped out from the shadows of the bushes.

"I told you I'd be here," I said.

"I came prepared." She picked up a heavy thermos, unscrewed the lid, and poured us both a cup of hot chocolate. "I should have brought something cold, but I gotta have my morning cocoa."

"Thanks," I looked at Marissa with a mixture of feelings. She was thoughtful, and smart, and ready to take on anything. Too bad she had to take on something as nasty as werewolves. Thinking about that made me angry—not just at the Wolves, but at Marissa, too, and I didn't understand why. So instead of thinking about it, I forced all my attention back to target practice.

"Time to shoot me some tree," I said, then put down the cup and picked up the crossbow, looking around for a likely target. About fifty yards away, I saw an ancient oak with a dark circle on its bark where a branch once had been, and an even darker spot near the center of the circle. A natural target. "That's my bull's-eye."

My quiver of arrows was slung over my shoulder, the way all professional merry men carry it. Without looking, I smoothly reached back for an arrow . . . and jabbed my finger on one of the sharp arrowheads. "Youch!" I put my finger in my mouth to suck the droplet of blood that appeared. Marissa grimaced.

"Note to self," I said with a laugh, "arrows go in point down."

Marissa chuckled.

Gingerly, I grasped an arrow by its shaft and pulled it out.

Then I placed it in the groove of the crossbow and pulled it back until the bowline was taut and the arrow locked into place.

I stared down the arrow with one eye closed, aiming at my victim tree until the sharp arrowhead pointed dead center, then I squeezed the trigger.

With a sharp hiss, the arrow was away. I followed its lightning-fast flight, so smooth, so quick—and so far off the mark. The arrow missed the tree by a good ten feet and landed somewhere in the bushes twenty yards beyond, stirring up a flock of pigeons.

"Nice shot, Robin Hood," Marissa said drily. "I think you just killed two birds with one arrow."

"I meant to do that," I said, pulling another arrow out of my quiver.

"I'll tell them to put that on your tombstone."

I gave her the cold look of a not-so-merry man and lined up my next shot. This time I held my breath as I pulled the trigger.

Thwack! The arrow hit the tree! Okay, so it wasn't anywhere near the target, but it was actually stuck in the tree I was aiming for.

"Nice," Marissa said, and I could tell by her tone that she really meant it.

I aimed my next shot high, and actually got the arrow closer to the circle. My next arrow was inside the outer ring of the target.

"I think maybe I just found my sport," I said, after firing the last of my arrows. "Too bad it took a battle with supernatural evil to find it."

We walked together to the tree to retrieve the arrows.

"I hope you *have* found your sport," Marissa said, suddenly intense. "I hope you can hit that bull's-eye again and again. Maybe . . ."

Her voice trailed off.

"Maybe what?"

She spoke so softly I could barely hear her voice. "Maybe that will save him."

"Save who?" I asked, knowing full well who she meant, but wanting to hear her say it.

"Marvin."

I nodded in understanding. Now I knew why this battle was so important to her. She saw it as a battle for Marvin's soul. She wanted to destroy all the Wolves before Marvin got bit and was turned into one.

"Come on," I said. We had reached the tree, and I grabbed the shafts sticking out of the bark. "We've got time for a few more rounds. You want to try?"

"No thanks," she said. "My taste in weapons is a little less . . . medieval. Your grandma's been taking me out to the firing range. We're not using silver bullets, of course, but the principle's the same."

I shot through the quiver of arrows three more times before I began to get paranoid that one of the Wolves might wander into the park and find us. Only about half my shots hit the tree. I knew with a few more weeks of practice I'd be much better. The problem was, I didn't have a few more weeks. I had only three more days.

"I don't know, Red, it's like your heart isn't really in it."

"Of course it is," I told her, and to prove it I fired three more shots. All three nailed the tree.

I went over to Grandma's house to report on my progress that night. She was proud of me, but I could tell she was worried about me, too—and in more ways than one.

She listened without saying a word as I told about my early-morning session with the crossbow. When I was done she stared at me for a long time, thinking. Finally, just as the silence was about to turn uncomfortable, she nodded her head.

"You're doing good, Red," she said. "You're proving yourself every day."

There was a mold on the dining-room table, holding about fifteen silver bullets.

"That's the last of them," Grandma said. "I've melted down every bit of silver in the house, and a whole bunch I got from the neighbors." She glanced up at me. "Will you be seeing Marissa tomorrow?" she asked. "She couldn't come by tonight."

I nodded. "She's meeting me at practice again in the morning."

Grandma went over to the cabinet next to the dining-room table and pulled out a drawer.

"Here." She reached in and lifted out a paper bag, handing it to me. It was heavy, and I could hear something rattling around inside.

"There are thirty silver bullets in there."

All at once I felt queasy, but if I got pale, Grandma didn't notice.

"Give them to Marissa when you see her," she said.

"All thirty?"

"She'll need as many bullets as she can get, come the night of the hunt."

The night of the hunt. It was getting real. This last week had flown by way too fast, and I don't know about Grandma and Marissa, but I didn't feel prepared.

I was back in the park for more crossbow practice the next morning—a drizzly dawn where it was hard to spot the tree through the mist. Marissa met me there, and I held up the paper bag Grandma had given me.

She looked at the pile of silver bullets inside the bag and shivered.

"That's a lot of silver," she said. "But it's not just about the ammo. I'm hoping I have what it takes to use them."

I nodded, trying not to show her how scared I was, too.

I set the bag on the grass, on top of my jacket, and picked up the crossbow.

I went through the quiver quickly. I was getting better. More arrows were hitting the tree, more were closer to the target. I even hit the bull's-eye once.

Marissa's curiosity got the better of her, and she finally tried the crossbow herself. She was just as bad as I had been when I first started.

I practiced long past when I should have stopped, but I was making real progress, and what were the chances that one of the Wolves would stumble upon us? The park was so overgrown, you could barely see us from the street.

It was midmorning when the arrow slipped.

It was careless. I had just locked the last arrow into the crossbow and hadn't aimed it yet when my finger accidentally hit the trigger. Marissa and I watched in shock as the arrow went flying out of the park. We heard a crash of glass, then the blaring car alarm.

Marissa bounded through the bushes, retrieved the arrow from the car's interior, and came running back. She laughed when she saw my stricken face.

"Don't worry," she said. "You didn't kill anybody. But you have to be more careful."

"Well, I'm done for today anyway," I said, walking with her to the tree to retrieve the rest of the arrows.

Then we heard the voices.

"Over here." It was A/C. "It's this one."

"Hey, the window's broken, but the stereo's still inside." It was Warhead.

"Grab it."

Marissa and I glanced at each other. My hand was already closing on the arrows in the tree.

"Hey—someone's coming!" I heard Loogie shout.

"So what? We didn't do it," said Marvin.

"Yeah, but *they* don't know that!"

And then I heard the worst sound I could possibly hear: The four of them were rustling through the bushes, coming into the park to hide, and headed straight for us.

14
ADVISER TO THE GODFATHER

I quickly yanked the arrows out of the bark and handed them to Marissa, along with the crossbow. I slipped the quiver off my shoulder and handed that to her as well.

"Get in the bushes!" I said softly. "Deep."

She nodded and ducked as far as she could under the shrubs, just as A/C, Warhead, Marvin, and Loogie came into view.

"Well, well, he's here after all!" said Marvin, almost snarling at me.

"I see him," said A/C. "Took long enough to track you down."

Track me down?

"What's the matter?" I said. "Can't a guy take a walk?"

We were all standing next to the tree I was using for target practice. A/C crossed his arms and leaned against it. "That's it?" he asked me. "Just taking a walk? Nothing else going on?"

A/C's shoulder was just a few inches from the bark that was riddled with holes from the arrows. He hadn't noticed them yet. How could he not notice them, they looked like giant black holes to me!

I moved away from the tree, but kept eye contact with him. "What else would be going on? It's getting closer to the full moon, and I'm kind of antsy, like I can't sit still, so I figured I'd take a walk."

"I hear you," A/C said, nodding. "Anyway, Cedric wants to see you. He thinks you're avoiding him."

"Avoiding him? No way."

Warhead was to my right, directly in front of the bush Marissa was hiding under. He sniffed the air suspiciously, and I suddenly had an awful thought.

"Uh . . . by the way, how'd you find me here?" I asked.

A/C pointed at his nose. "A werewolf's nose is his best friend—especially this close to the full moon."

Warhead was still sniffing. He knew someone else had been here. Marvin might not have been a werewolf yet, but if he got close enough, I'll bet he'd recognize his sister's perfume. If they found her with the crossbow and arrows, it would be all over for us. So thinking fast, I said, "Hey, Marvin—you just missed your sister."

Warhead stopped sniffing, and Marvin snapped his eyes to me, glaring. "What was she doing here?"

I matched his glare. "Like I said, we were taking a walk."

Then a corner of his mouth turned up in a smirk. "Looks like she finally wised up and ditched you."

I wanted to match insult for insult, but I had to hold back that urge. Getting Marissa out of mind, if not out of scent, was more important. I looked down and shrugged, like maybe he was right. His smirk widened into a full-fledged gloat, so I burped in his face, figuring that would get his mind off it, and kill any other scent as well.

"Yuck!" He pushed me away from him, hard.

Warhead laughed, and A/C straightened up. Only Loogie didn't seem to react. He was busy covering his eyes from the weak glare of the sun, which was just peeking over the tops of the nearby buildings.

"Sun's getting high," Loogie said as he moved closer to a tree to get under the shadow. "It's gonna be another scorcher. We should get back to the Hollow."

"What's the matter?" I asked. "Can't take the heat?"

"No," Loogie said, slipping on his sunglasses. "I just don't got my sunscreen, that's all."

I laughed. Loogie was about as white as a corpse in Clorox—and seemed even paler than he used to be, now that he was set against the rich greens and browns of the park. "Ain't ever heard of a werewolf that needs sunscreen," I said. His skin was practically translucent—like you could see right through it to his veins.

"Now you have."

I wondered if that would affect his fur as a werewolf . . . then I realized that I would know the answer very soon.

"Come on," said A/C. "Cedric's waiting."

"Okay. Let me get my jacket."

"Whaddaya need a jacket for in this heat?"

"It was raining when I got here." And then I silently cursed myself. It hadn't been raining since dawn. That fact was lost on everyone except for Marvin. He glared at me.

"How early were you out 'walking' with my sister?"

"Early enough not to be bothered by you."

Marvin glared at me some more, but that was okay, because it kept his attention away from the target tree, riddled with arrow holes.

As we walked away from the tree, I figured I'd make a narrow escape . . . until I reached the spot where I'd left my jacket on the ground.

There was a bag of silver bullets sitting on top it, and it was wide open.

How could I have been so stupid? One glance down from any of them and they would see what was inside.

"Hang on," I said, bending over it. I quickly rolled up the top of the bag and tossed it gently aside, trying to make it look like I was just adding a new piece of litter to the litter-ridden park. Then I picked up my jacket and turned to go.

"What about the bag?" A/C asked.

"Is there food inside?" Warhead asked. "If you don't want it, I'll eat it. I'm starved." He tried to pick it up, but I got to it first.

"Nothing you'd like," I told him, holding it out of his reach.

"Hey—you were throwing it away," Warhead said. "Now you're keeping it, just so I can't have it?"

"C'mon," said A/C impatiently, "just take it and let's go."

And so without any other choice, I took the bag of bullets meant for Marissa and left the park.

We pushed our way through the hedge surrounding the park and headed in the direction of Troll Bridge Hollow. As we walked, I rolled the top of the paper bag down even tighter, to pack the bullets down so they wouldn't rattle. Marvin must have seen the way I was clutching it, because he snatched it away.

"Did Grandma pack her Little Red lunch?"

I grabbed it back from him before he could look inside. "No, your sister did, and sealed it with a kiss."

Marvin tried to slug me, but A/C held him back. "Touch him and you answer to Cedric," A/C said.

Marvin snorted at that. "This little snot's got you all wrapped around his finger, and you just let him do it."

At the next corner, I wanted to drop the bag casually into a trash can, figuring I could come back and get it later, but Warhead still had his eyes on it and wanted a bite of whatever it was he thought I had. I knew I'd have to keep the bullets with me.

A/C and Warhead turned a corner up ahead, and Loogie was somewhere far behind. Suddenly I felt a hand digging into my shoulder. It was Marvin. He stopped me before I turned the corner.

"You know Cedric doesn't control me like he controls the others." He spoke quietly, so only I would be able to hear him. "I don't play by his rules. Any agreements between you and him don't mean anything to me. You got that?"

I started to answer him, but he cut me off. "No, don't say anything. Just keep looking straight ahead." He prodded me forward, and I kept walking. When we turned the corner, A/C and Warhead were twenty feet ahead of us.

"So," Marvin continued, "Cedric promised you he'd leave your grandmother alone? Well, that's Cedric's business. But I make no such promises. I politely asked you to keep your paws away from my sister, but you didn't. So now your dear sweet grandma and the rest of your family move to the top of my dinner menu."

Then he chuckled. It was a low, unpleasant sound. And when he was through chuckling, he said, "That is, they *would* be on the menu . . . if I were a werewolf."

We arrived at the Hollow. Cedric was waiting, and I could tell that he was already feeling the effects of the growing moon. His jaw was set like stone, a vein pulsed on his neck, and he was pacing like a caged animal in the dreary depths of that dim chamber. The entire place was already starting to smell like animal musk and dog breath. Each night, as it got closer to the full moon, they were all changing just a little bit inside—and although I knew it was just my imagination, I felt like I was changing, too. Without even realizing it, I reached to my chest and felt the Saint Gabriel's coin that was still hanging from my neck, hiding beneath my shirt. *Protection,* I thought. I wondered if it could protect me from myself.

"I want to know where you've been!" Cedric demanded when he saw me. "And why you haven't been reporting to me all you know about the hunters."

I forced myself to be calm, answering in an easy tone of voice. "I've been gathering information," I told him. "No sense reporting back until I had something worth telling."

Cedric relaxed the tiniest bit. "You got something?"

"Oh, yeah!" I smiled, and didn't say anything more for a few long seconds, keeping him in suspense. I noticed Cedric glancing down at the bag in my hand, so I spoke up, pulling his attention away from the bag and back to me.

"The hunters know about Troll Bridge Hollow," I said.

"Because you told them!" shouted Marvin.

"Shut your face!" Cedric said, then turned back to me. "So how do they know?"

"It's not too hard a thing to find out. I'll bet they've known for a long time." I told him, "This isn't a good place to get caught—only one entrance with no back door. They're gonna have sharpshooters posted in a nearby building. They're gonna pick us off one by one as we come out the door tomorrow night."

The others looked worried, but Cedric just smiled. "And how do they know we're gonna be here?"

I smiled right back. "I told them I'd make sure of it."

Cedric nodded. "So they think we're gonna be like ducks in a shooting gallery. Are all the hunters gonna be here?"

"Every last one of them."

"Let's go take care of them now," said Warhead, pounding his fist into his palm.

"We'll wait till we go wolfing." Cedric crossed his arms. "What kind of weapons they got?"

"State-of-the-art," I told him. "Automatic rifles with laser sights. You see a little pinprick of red, and the next moment you're history."

"Silver bullets?"

And then I had a brainstorm. There was already too much interest in the bag I was holding. I knew I wouldn't get out of there without someone seeing inside . . . but maybe the truth could set me free.

"Yeah, they've got silver bullets," I said. "But a lot fewer than they think they have." Then I emptied the bag on the table right in front of Cedric. A few bullets rolled onto the floor, and the Wolves jumped back like they were acid.

"You stole these from your own grandmother?" Cedric laughed and laughed. "You are one bad little wolverine!"

"You got that right!"

He looked at the bullets—I could see a little bit of fear in his face, and Cedric never showed fear. "Okay—get rid of them."

So I did. I picked up all the silver bullets and put them back in the bag. "I'll go up on the bridge and throw them into the river," I said.

"We have to leave Troll Bridge Hollow; we can't stay here," said A/C, looking to Cedric for approval. "We should pick up and move, right now."

"Don't be dumb! That would be too suspicious," I told him. "You gotta pretend like you don't know anything. You can't let them know that you're onto them."

"Exactly," said Cedric.

I pointed to a grate on the ground toward the back of the huge room. "Anyone know what's down there?"

"Just a drainage tunnel," said Klutz. "It empties out into the river."

"There's our back door," I said.

"Good thinking," said Cedric. "We'll get everyone here before sundown—then, once we transform, we'll get out through the tunnel, sneak up on the hunters from behind, and it's supper time." Then Cedric turned back to me. "You gave us all the information we needed," he said. "Your job is done."

I didn't like the sound of that. "Cool," I said, rolling up the lip on the bag of silver bullets. "I'll go get rid of these." I turned to go, and then Cedric did something that I wasn't expecting.

"I'll go with you," he said.

The last thing that I wanted right then was to be alone with Cedric, but I wasn't about to let him know that. Maybe he just wanted to walk me up, to make sure I got rid of those bullets— if I were him, that's what I would do. But then he could have sent any one of the Wolves to do that, he didn't have to come himself. I had given him all the information he needed. It meant I wasn't needed anymore. I began to wonder if it was going to be me, instead of the bullets, that got thrown off the bridge.

I swallowed hard and tried to pretend like I wasn't scared.

A set of rusty metal service stairs zigzagged up the side of the Troll Bridge Hollow to the bridge deck above. Halfway up, Cedric stopped me. We were in darkness, and in the shadow cast by the bridge, no one could see us. I could barely see him.

"You talked like a real know-it-all in there," he said. "You made everyone else look foolish."

"I . . . uh . . . I didn't mean to," I said. "I was just trying to be sensible."

"Sensible," he echoed. I couldn't figure out if his voice was mocking. "A/C's my second in command, and I don't think he liked that you talked back to him, calling him dumb."

"Like I said—"

"Yeah, I know," Cedric said. "You were being sensible."

Cedric was quiet for a moment, then he said, "Did you ever watch any of those Mafia movies?"

I had to laugh—what did that have to do with anything? "Like, which ones?"

"Any of them. All of them. There's TV shows, too. See, it's always the same—there's the head guy. He's the boss, or the Godfather, or whatever. He's got lieutenants and captains and stuff. It's like a friggin' army."

"Yeah? So?" The bullets were feeling heavier and heavier in my hands.

"There's always this one guy, though. The *consigliere*. Ever hear of that?"

"I don't think so."

"You know what it is?"

"No," I said.

Cedric rapped me on the shoulder. "See—so you're not a complete know-it-all." I let out a nervous little laugh. Cedric continued. "The *consigliere* is like the adviser to the Godfather. Kind of like his second in command, without *really* being his second in command."

I took a deep breath, suddenly realizing where this was going.

"See," said Cedric, "A/C is gonna be the first of us heading out. He's going to Chicago, and I'm going to need to appoint someone else to be second in command. But it can't be you, because that's gonna tick off the other guys. *'Why's he making the Wolverine second in charge?'* they're gonna say, and they ain't gonna listen to you—heck, if I were them I wouldn't listen to a snot-nosed brat like you, either. But, see, you got the brains that they don't have, and they're all too stupid to see it. So there's no way you can be second in command," he said again. "But that doesn't mean you can't be *consigliere*."

He waited for me to respond, but I didn't, because I just didn't know what to feel. I was relieved that he didn't come up here to kill me, and stupefied that he was willing to put so much faith in me, when I was really the enemy.

"So tomorrow we take care of the hunters, then the next night, you'll get 'made.' After your first kill, we'll talk about it." He patted me on the shoulder. "So are we gonna toss these bullets?"

"Sure," I said, but my voice came out little more than a whisper. "I'll take care of it."

"You're doing good, Red," he said. "You're proving yourself every day." Then he turned and clattered back down the stairs.

The sound of his footsteps faded, and I continued up until I reached the deck of the bridge. Cars whizzed past, not knowing or caring that I was there, as I followed the bridge's walkway, until I was halfway across the river. I looked over the edge, holding the bag of bullets. I knew I could take them to Marissa, and the Wolves would never know. Simple as that. Simple. But instead I found myself hurling the bag, bullets and all, over the edge of the bridge, and into the water.

15

PREGNANT MOON

You did WHAT with the bullets?" Grandma shouted.

I had walked around for hours before I worked up enough nerve to go to Grandma's house. It was evening by the time I got there.

I didn't mean to tell her how it happened. I started out just telling her the bullets were lost, but Grandma has a way of poking and prodding at the loose ends of a story until the whole thing just unravels.

"The Wolves trust me. I had to prove myself worthy to them—they were all watching me!" It was a lie. No one had been watching. I told myself that I had a good reason for lying to Grandma, but that was just a lie, too.

"Listen," I told her. "I've got some information for you." Then I told her how the Wolves planned to sneak out through the drainage tunnel beneath Troll Bridge Hollow. "Find where that tunnel lets out, and you'll have them," I said.

Grandma sized me up for a moment, then said calmly, "That information can't help us if we don't have silver bullets," she said. "But I suppose you already knew that."

"I'm sorry," I said. "I'm really, really sorry."

Grandma looked at me, stared into my eyes, and said nothing. Then, finally, she smiled. "Of course you're sorry. I know you are."

Only there was no warmth in her smile, and her eyes were still hard.

"What are you going to do now?" I asked her.

"Oh, don't you worry about that. I'll cook up something."

"Hey—you had some other bullets, didn't you?" I asked. "The ones that were still cooling? Where did you put them?"

"Someplace safe," she said quickly, almost sharply, and didn't bother to tell me where.

I reached to my chest, feeling the little silver coin that Mom had given me. It wasn't much, but it could be melted down into a single bullet.

"Maybe I could give you some silver, Grandma."

"Don't worry, Red. I'll manage. I always have."

It was as though a chill had descended on the room. Grandma moved around the house, locking cabinets and drawers, as if absentmindedly. But she didn't miss a single one.

"Are you worried about me, Grandma?" I asked.

"Oh, not at all, not at all," she said. "I'm sure you know exactly what you're doing. Why don't you run along home now, Red. I have a lot to do, a lot to prepare."

"Grandma, please, let me help you."

But I could see a guarded expression on her face now, a look of suspicion that I had never seen there before.

"No, you've been enough help, I think."

I went home and tried to sleep, but couldn't, so I stared up at the moon, watching how it's trailing edge faded into darkness, so close to being full, but not quite there. A pregnant moon, Grandma called it. Full almost to bursting, and ready to give birth to something unthinkable. Tomorrow night, the Wolves would prowl the city streets, devouring anyone in their path. Tomorrow night would also change my life forever. Whatever happened tomorrow, whichever way it went down, I know nothing would ever be the same.

When my alarm went off before dawn, I got out of bed and went down to the park, but Marissa never showed. A little later I tried calling Grandma, to offer my help again, but there was no answer.

I spent the day in a kind of fog. I couldn't think straight, couldn't make any decisions. I felt paralyzed as I waited for the sun to set.

I went by the antique shop at five o'clock. A sign on the door said BACK IN FIFTEEN MINUTES, but the back door was unlocked, so I let myself in.

"Marissa," I called softly. "Are you here?"

There was no answer, so I sat down behind the register to wait.

And that's when I noticed the box on the counter by the register. It was a small, thin box, the kind that usually holds a watch or a bracelet, the kind of gift girls go gaga over.

Except this one didn't have a girl's name on it. It had mine.

I picked up the box. It didn't have any gift wrap or ribbon on it, just a piece of tape holding it closed, and another piece of tape holding the small envelope with my name on it.

I tore open the envelope and found a note.

YOU AIN'T TOO SHARP, RED.
YOURS TRULY, MARVIN.

I lifted the lid off the box. Inside was a tarnished silver butter knife.

What was it supposed to mean? Was it a threat? Not a very scary one. *You ain't too sharp.* Was the dull knife just a joke, or was there something I wasn't getting here? Was there something about the knife itself?

I held the tarnished knife up to the light and studied it. It was heavy, thick, with a finely detailed pattern of flowers on the handle. I turned the blade over and noticed some printing on the flat side of the blade, near the handle. The words *stainless steel.*

It was just a cheap, steel butter knife, not an expensive silver one.

But stainless steel doesn't tarnish—that's something that happens only to silver. I looked at the knife again, scratched it with my thumbnail, and the stains came off on my fingers. Silver tarnish won't do that, you have to use special polish. So this knife wasn't tarnished at all—but it had been "antiqued." Someone had brushed it with steel wool and used special acids to make it appear like silver. People who didn't know the difference would think they were getting something of value.

A thought started to roll around in the back of my head. I put the knife down on the counter and stood up, feeling a little dizzy.

I looked across the store at the crowded shelf of knick-knacks and spotted the silver candelabra Marissa had used to find out whether or not Marvin was a werewolf.

I walked over to the shelf and stood in front of the heavy object. Five curlicue branches arched out from the center. The tarnished silver gleamed dully under the display light of the cabinet.

I didn't want to, but I reached out and picked it up. Then I scratched the base with my thumbnail. The "tarnish" came right off.

The candelabra wasn't silver at all. It was steel, treated to look like silver.

Which meant Marvin never touched silver . . .

A sharp slam of pain knocked the thought out of my mind, and my head was once again filled with cartoon stars before everything went black.

I woke up so sore I couldn't move. Then I realized I couldn't move because my arms were bound together behind my back. I tried to stand, but my ankles were tied to the chair, so I tried to cry out, but couldn't do that, either. Something stuffed in my mouth kept me from making a sound.

The Wolves must have been in the antique store, waiting for me! But why? I thought they trusted me.

Marvin . . . there was something about Marvin I needed to remember. Something I had found out . . .

I saw something moving out of the corner of my eye and turned my head to look. Big mistake. I felt a sharp pain radiating from where I had been hit on the head, and I groaned.

"He's awake," a voice said. It was cold as ice, but it wasn't a voice I expected. It was Marissa. She and Grandma came over to where I sat.

"We had to do this for your own good," Grandma said. "I'm sorry, Red."

I shook my head vigorously, in spite of the pain.

Marvin . . . something important about Marvin. Why can't I remember?

"Really, Red," Grandma went on, "I'm sorry. You're not a Wolf yet, and I won't let them make you one—even if it's what you *think* you want. Once we get rid of all the Wolves, you'll be out of danger and we'll let you go."

Then I saw the stainless-steel butter knife sitting on the counter, and I remembered everything.

Marvin! He never touched silver! We have no proof that he's not a werewolf—which means he probably is *one!*

"Mrrrvmmm! Mrrvmmm uh wrrrwrrrffl!" It was no use! I tried to spit out the gag so my words would make sense. I hadn't even told them that I had done the job and had set the Wolves up for the trap we were going to spring. We. It wasn't we anymore—I had just been cut out of the whole thing, which meant Marissa and Grandma were going alone. Our chances were bad enough with three—but two?

Frustrated and furious, I shook the ropes that held my arms behind my back, trying to get loose.

"Give it up," said Marissa. "You're not going anywhere."

She looked at me like she hated me. The way Marvin had always looked at me. I stopped struggling and stared at her, trying to send her a message with my eyes. Trying to let her know I had something important to tell her.

The message didn't go through. Marissa turned away.

"Come on," Grandma said to her. "We've still got a lot to do, and there's not a whole lot of time left. The moon's just short of rising."

They left me sitting there, trussed up like a Thanksgiving turkey. I could hear them in another part of the shop getting their equipment together. I had to get through to Grandma somehow. I tried to calm down and think. My hands were tied behind me, my ankles were tied to the legs of the chair, but the chair itself wasn't tied down.

I inched forward in the chair, putting all my weight over one of the front legs as I scraped it against the floor. It left a faint, but visible line. I inched the chair back, then forward, then back again, and looked down. Clear as day, I had etched the letter *M* into the wood floor!

While I worked, I could hear Grandma and Marissa talking.

"You have the ammo?" I heard Marissa ask.

"All that's left of it. Fifteen bullets. I'll have to make them count. Good thing you thought of the balloons. Do you have them?"

"Right here," Marissa answered.

I paused for a second. Balloons? What was that about? I kept working on scraping out my message. *M . . . A . . . R . . . V . . .*

I had gotten to the first *R* in *werewolf* when Grandma came back into the room. She had on a leather jacket, biker pants, and a helmet. Her face and hands were covered with mud, to hide her scent. She looked as far from being my crazy old grandmother as could be.

"We're going now, Red. You'll be safe here." Although wolfsbane would have been too suspicious a smell for them to have, Grandma did light some wolfsbane incense for me and left it on the counter. "Sit tight and we'll let you go when it's all over." Then she sighed. "And . . . and if we don't make it back . . . well . . . someone will be here in the morning."

I groaned and tilted my head, pointed my toes, and did everything I could to get her to look down at what I had scratched on the floor.

MARVIN WEREW

If she saw it, I knew she'd take the gag out of my mouth to let me explain. I kept looking at her then staring down at the floor, her, then the floor over and over again. Finally I knew I had her attention! She came over to me, and I knew she was going to take the gag out of my mouth!

But I was wrong. She just adjusted it.

I looked at her, and to the floor again, and she misread that gesture of my eyes.

"Feeling ashamed, Red?"

I looked to the floor once more, but she just didn't get it. "I was counting on your help tonight . . . but to go over to the other side?" She backed away. "Maybe you *should* feel ashamed."

She turned and left without once looking down at the floor. Marissa, also covered with protective leather, was right behind her. She glared at me on her way out.

I could see a tiny bit of the front window from where I was sitting. I could see the sky had turned to night. And at the very edge of the visible piece of window, I could just make out the bright curvature of the full moon. While I was sitting there tied up, it had risen, and somewhere, far off in the distance, I heard the night's first howl.

I had to get out of there!

As I shifted my position to try to get a better sense of how high the moon was in the sky, I saw the stainless-steel butter knife on the counter. Marvin's terrible gift to me. I scraped my chair over to the counter, then used my chin to push the butter knife to the floor. I took a deep breath, closed my eyes, and tipped over sideways until the chair fell. I tried to take most of the impact with my shoulder, but I still felt a sharp stab of pain in my head, where Marissa had conked me. The world started to go dark, but I struggled to remain conscious.

I scrambled around and felt blindly behind my back until I had the butter knife in my hands.

A butter knife has a dull blade, not the best edge for cutting a rope—but it *is* a knife. I rubbed the cords holding my wrists together over the butter knife again and again for at least fifteen minutes before I finally felt the bindings starting to give. After a few more minutes I managed to pull my wrists apart.

I rubbed them a few times to get the circulation moving, then untied my feet from the chair legs. Staggering to the door of the shop, I stared out onto the moonlit pavement. I heard another howl, not so far away this time.

Grandma and Marissa were out there somewhere. So were Cedric and the Wolves.

A battle to the death.

It was up to me to tip the scales one way or the other.

Bring it on.

16
▲
SILVER CITY

Hardly a cloud dared to touch the sky on this terrible night. The full moon shining over the city gave every surface an eerie silver sheen. There's an old-fashioned kind of photograph Grandma had once told me about. It's called a *daguerreotype*. She had a couple of them hanging on her walls. Instead of the photo being printed on paper, it was printed onto the surface of a mirror, so instead of black and white it was all black and silver. The whole city was a daguerreotype tonight.

My bike was still propped up behind the antique shop, and I rode it at breakneck speed through the silver city, skidding around corners, crisscrossing through alleys that I knew would shave a few seconds off my ride. My hands and feet were numb from fear being pumped through my veins, as deadly as nitroglycerine. My whole body felt like a bomb ticking down to detonation.

You can't imagine what it's like to be torn between darkness and light—to be a traitor no matter what move you make. If my grandmother and Marissa died tonight, it would be because

I had stayed in the darkness too long, flirting with the idea of being Cedric's *consigliere*. If that happened, I could never live with myself—but if Cedric gave me the bite as he planned, I would be forced to live with it forever. That was the worst hell I could imagine.

I knew where the Wolves were and the not-so-secret drainage-tunnel exit they'd be trying to slip out of by the river, just above the waterline. They expected to double back to Troll Bridge Hollow and surprise the two dozen hunters they thought were waiting for them. Little did they know that it was just Grandma and Marissa, waiting in ambush as they came out of the drainage tunnel. I had no idea what I would do when I got there, only that I had to go.

I was about two blocks from Troll Bridge Hollow when I heard gunshots and the Wolves going crazy. Howling, yipping, screaming in frenzy.

I pedaled harder, pushing my bike to the max, and covered the last blocks in seconds. I turned the corner, misjudged, and took it too fast. The bike skidded out from under me, and I scraped across the pavement on my back and shoulders.

I rolled over into a low crouch and paused there, catching my breath and taking a good look around at my surroundings.

I was down by the edge of the river, just a dozen yards away from the drainage tunnel, but the Wolves were nowhere to be seen. No—that wasn't entirely true. There were three furry masses lying motionless on the rocks near the tunnel. It looked like the ambush had worked, but not as well as Grandma and Marissa had intended. It made me feel both frightened and relieved, and the two feelings battled inside me. I hurried back up Troll Street, listening for the sound of howls, or shots.

The buildings facing the bridge were dark. I trotted toward a doorway, planning to crouch there until I caught my breath, but I had only made it halfway when I heard a wolf howl somewhere unseen, a block or so away. The howl was followed by a gunshot, then a yip of pain, followed by more howling and growling from others.

I took a deep breath and ran for the corner, staying low. One more wolf down. How many bullets had Grandma already used up? How many did she have left? And who'd been taken out already? I immediately hoped it wasn't A/C, or Klutz . . . or Cedric.

No! I told myself, pressing my knuckles to my forehead until it hurt. *I can't let myself think that way. They're not people. Not now. They're wolves.* Yet every single death cry tore into me like a wolf claw. I reached the side street and turned the corner. There was the downed wolf, lying in the street. I could see it was writhing in pain, then it breathed its last.

Pressing close to the buildings, I passed the dead wolf's position. I looked a moment too long, because I recognized something in the set of its muzzle. It was Warhead.

I could hear howls starting up again, halfway down the block. I stepped away from the building toward the center of the sidewalk so I could see farther down the street.

Three wolves were chasing after someone. It was too small to be Grandma. It was Marissa—and she had my crossbow. She was running from the wolves, but they were gaining on her. She spun around and fired an arrow at them, but it went wide. Then I saw her reaching for something in her backpack.

She flung a small round object at the wolves on her heels.

A water balloon.

The balloon exploded on the lead wolf's nose. The animal screamed and flopped over, rubbing its face against the street, trying to wipe whatever it was off. The other two wolves stopped and looked fearfully at the dying wolf, then at each other, as Marissa kept running.

A gunshot came from above, and another one of the wolves went down. *That must have come from Grandma,* I thought.

The third wolf took off in my direction, barking like mad. I couldn't tell if it was warning the others away or calling them to battle.

As it ran toward me, I stepped back into a doorway. It ran past without seeing me, and I prayed it didn't smell me.

After the wolf passed, I ran after Marissa. I had to warn her about her brother.

I passed by the dead wolves lying in the street. From the one that Marissa had hit with the balloon I recognized a familiar smell from Grandma's darkroom. It was silver bromide—the kind they coat photographic paper with. The same chemical that killed Grandpa. Marissa had filled water balloons with a silver-bromide solution.

I got to the intersection at the end of the block, but I didn't see Marissa, and I had no idea in which direction she had run.

Then I heard a scream.

I ran toward the sound, legs pumping hard, breath coming out in spurts.

As I turned the corner, I saw Marissa in the middle of the street, running back toward me. Two werewolves were coming up behind her. Then two more sprang from the alleyway, directly in her path, and she stopped short. Now she was surrounded by four wolves.

She struggled with the crossbow, trying to load an arrow, but in her panic she dropped the whole bow. It was still clattering on the street as she reached into her pack and pulled out two water balloons, holding them, circling warily. I kept on running toward them, but I was still too far away to do anything.

Now the Wolves were barking at her, snarling and snapping their jaws, but none of them were willing to be the first to attack—the first to get the lethal liquid thrown in their faces. It was a standoff, and something had to give soon.

Three more wolves joined the circle. It wouldn't be long now before one of them made a move. They kept circling Marissa and barking at her, daring to take a step closer each time.

Then I realized that there was something I could do. I had told Cedric and the others that the hunters had laser sights on their rifles. At the time it had just been a detail I made up to make the story about the hunters seem real. I had no idea how important that little detail would become. I reached down to my key chain and grabbed my laser pointer. Then I ducked into the shadows of a doorway, aimed the laser pointer at the wolf pack, and pushed the button.

A tiny red circle suddenly appeared on the side of one of the wolves, and the wolf next to him barked out a warning and leaped out of the way. The wolf marked with the red spot of light froze, then crouched and rolled, yipping in fear.

The others, sensing a problem in their ranks, looked away

from Marissa for just a second—and that was all the time she needed. She threw the balloons at the two closest wolves and then leaped over them and out of the center of the circle.

I aimed my laser pointer again and again. Each time the red spot landed on a wolf, the wolf would run in circles, scared to death.

Then a gunshot rang out. It must have been Grandma, firing from her position. One of the wolves fell, and that was all it took to confirm to the rest that the red laser was attached to a rifle scope.

The pack scattered, and I ran for the crossbow Marissa had dropped in the street. As I dove for it, a motorcycle roared to life and came screaming out of the alley on its rear tire. The biker leaned forward, dropping the front tire to the road, and spun around next to me. The headlight was blinding, and I had to put my hand over my eyes to shield them from the glare.

It was Grandma! She looked bigger than life, like an action-movie hero, steering with one hand, holding her pistol in the other at arm's length.

She had the gun aimed directly at a wolf that was baring its fangs at her, snarling. I couldn't be sure, but something about its expression made me think it was A/C.

She took aim, unaware that directly behind her another wolf was getting ready to pounce. It opened its mouth wide, and I saw a glint of gold. It was Marvin!

"Grandma!" I screamed as Marvin started his leap. "No!"

I reached her first and pulled her down off her bike. Her gun fired wild, the bullet ricocheting harmlessly off the building behind A/C. Marvin leaped over our heads, his slathering mouth right where Grandma's neck would have been if I hadn't grabbed her. I don't think she ever saw him—all she knew was that I had ruined her clean shot.

As Grandma and I were rolling on the street, Marvin scrambled to a stop, and A/C prepared to leap on us, but I spun around. From behind Grandma's back, I aimed my laser pointer at them, first at Marvin, then at A/C.

"Marvin! A/C!" I shouted from where I lay hidden. "Hunters!"

A/C and Marvin backpedaled, looking around wildly. They turned tail and ran the other way.

"Red!?" Grandma shouted at me when she finally caught her breath. "Are you trying to get me killed? Get out of my way!"

I had no time to explain what had really happened. I scrambled to my feet and ran in Marissa's direction. She was all by herself, and I was afraid she'd need help.

Sure enough, as I rounded the corner, I saw Marissa facing off with one of the wolves.

It was the biggest, meanest wolf yet. And I knew at once it was Cedric. It didn't matter that he was in wolf form, his profile was unmistakable, the sneer on his lips, the scorn in his eye.

I ran toward them, trying to aim the crossbow as I ran.

As Marissa raised her arm to throw a balloon at Cedric, and Cedric poised to leap on her, I screamed, "NO!"

I stopped running, took aim at a point between Cedric's eyes, and pulled the trigger.

The arrow flew straight and true, until it veered toward Marissa at the last second. Time seemed to slow down. I watched in horror and disbelief as the arrow came close to her, then whisked past her and out of sight, narrowly missing her forehead.

Marissa stumbled back a step, dropping the balloon. It seemed to float in midair for a second before plummeting to the pavement, where it burst, the chemical droplets splashing harmlessly on the ground.

Cedric turned and looked in my direction, his menacing snarl twisting into a cruel grin. He looked directly in my eyes and howled.

He knew at last whose side I was on, and it wasn't his!

Cedric turned back to face Marissa, ready to finish her off, but before he could move, another wolf leaped from the shadows, reaching toward Marissa with its gigantic jaws. Again I saw a glint of gold coming from the wolf's open mouth.

Marvin? Was Marvin going to devour his own sister!?

I had no more arrows, but I started running toward him anyway.

Marvin caught Marissa in his jaws, his huge mouth grabbing her by the waist, and he raced away with her. He ran down the street, carrying his sister, with Cedric right behind.

I chased them as far as I could, for about three blocks, but they were much too fast for me. I lost them.

Then I heard a gunning motorcycle directly behind me.

I turned around as Grandma caught up to me, looking at me with disbelief and fury.

"You tried to get me killed, Red. You're not even a Wolf yet, and you're serving me up to them!"

"That's not what happened, Grandma!"

"You're a traitor to your family!" She spat out the words. "I don't know you anymore. And I don't want to."

Grandma gunned her motorcycle and took off down the street, leaving me alone.

As soon as she was gone, I heard the sound of heavy paws running toward me down the street. I turned to face the werewolf. I had nothing to protect myself with, but I wasn't going to die without seeing my attacker.

The wolf ran at full speed in my direction. I looked around for anything to defend myself with, but had nothing. Then I remembered the arrow I had fired, the one that had narrowly missed Marissa. It was behind me in the street.

I turned and ran for it, sliding into the gutter as I grabbed the arrow.

I turned to face the wolf, holding up the crossbow and fumbling with the arrow as the wolf was nearly upon me, but I wasn't fast enough.

It leaped toward me—I braced for impact—but the wolf never came down.

Of all the crazy things I had seen that night, this was by far the craziest . . .

. . . because in midleap the werewolf began to change shape. It seemed to shrink in size, its wolf body collapsing to the size of a fox. Its front legs stretched, becoming flaps of skin, which turned into wings. Its rear legs and tail shrank to next to nothing.

The furry thing flapped its wings and sailed over my head. I craned my neck back to see where it was going. It flew crazily, as if it were just getting used to the feeling of flight, and then veered and took off to the north. I watched it until it flew out of sight behind a building.

I put my head back on the pavement and breathed out. I didn't even realize I had been holding my breath. I didn't want to think about what I had just seen, or what it meant. I just wanted to breathe in, and breathe out, assuring myself that I had made it through the battle, and that somehow I was still alive.

17

▲

CHUPACABRA

I holed up that night in an empty Dumpster—maybe the same one Marvin had tossed me into weeks before, I don't know. I didn't sleep. I couldn't. Marvin had Marissa, and who knew what he had done with her; Grandma had lost her faith in me, and I had betrayed the Wolves. Playing both sides left me with no sides. I was now everyone's enemy.

I didn't know what the morning would bring . . . but when the sun rose, birds took to the skies, the sounds of morning filled the air, and it was as if the insanity of the night before never happened. I crawled out of my Dumpster to a disgustingly normal day. Buses came and went, full of people on their way to work. Tina Soames was playing out in front of her apartment building with her friends.

I decided I'd go home, if just for a few minutes, to clean up and unscramble my brain. The surviving Wolves would all be sleeping off the night somewhere, which meant I had a little bit of time before they came after me.

When I got home, the phone was ringing. I let the machine pick it up.

"Red? Where are you?" It was my dad. He and Mom were the lucky ones, off on their carefree Mediterranean vacation. "We've been trying you for days. We've been trying your grandma. Is something wrong? Where are you?"

I had to pick up. "Hi, Dad," I said, trying to sound as normal as possible.

"Where have you been? We've been calling and calling!"

I gave them lots of one-word answers, which I had become pretty skilled at. "Fine . . . Good . . . Yeah . . . Fine . . . Okay . . ."

They were coming back in a week. How could I tell them that a week was as long as a lifetime now? "Great . . . Fine . . . Yeah . . . Miss you, too. Bye."

I took a shower, pretending that I could wash away the memory of last night along with the dirt. Then I made myself a bowl of canned soup, because it was the closest thing to "comfort food" I could find in the place. But before I could take a single spoonful, someone started pounding on the front door.

"Open up, Red! I know you're in there." It was Cedric.

Boom, Boom, Boom. The whole apartment shook with his pounding. I thought werewolves couldn't resist the urge to sleep after changing back to human! That's what Grandma had said. I had to think fast. I grabbed my mom's shower cap from the bathroom, and a pair of pink fuzzy slippers.

Boom, Boom, Boom.

I raced into my parents' room and pulled down the shades.

Boom, Boom, Boom.

I dove under the covers, pulling them tight around me.

Boom, Boom, CRASH! The front door tore loose and smashed to the ground. I heard Cedric stomping around, until he appeared, a large silhouette in the doorway.

"Red?"

"How dare you break into our home!" I said in a high-pitched voice. "Red's not here. Now go away, you hoodlum, before I call the police!"

Cedric slowly strode in. "So, you're Red's mother?"

"I said leave!"

Still Cedric strode closer. "My, my, ma'am. What big feet you have," he said. "You barely fit in those slippers of yours."

"I'm warning you—I have nine-one-one on auto-dial."

"My, my, ma'am," said Cedric. "What broad shoulders you have."

"Runs in the family. I'm picking up the phone."

I reached for the phone, but Cedric grabbed it first. "My, my, ma'am, what nail-bitten fingers you have."

"From worrying about my Little Red."

Cedric hurled the phone across the room. It shattered against the wall in a hundred pieces. Then he grabbed the covers, tore them off, and pulled off my shower cap.

"I knew it!" he said. "You're busted!"

I braced for the last and most painful moment of my life.

"After what you did last night you think you can just go back home, like nothing happened?"

I said nothing.

"You saved my life, man!" Cedric said. "That changes everything."

Saved his life? I was still speechless, but now for a whole different reason.

"The way you stopped Marvin's sister when she was about to silverize me. The way you knocked down your own grandma when she was about to get A/C. You showed true loyalty, man. True loyalty."

He thought I was shooting at Marissa! He had no idea I had been aiming at him. I couldn't believe it! I didn't know whether to laugh, or barf.

"You were right—there were dozens of hunters, coming after us from all directions. Little red laser spots everywhere! We should have been more careful."

I tried to speak, but my voice came out squeaky, like I was still imitating my mother. I cleared my throat and tried again. "How many Wolves did they get?"

"Too many." Cedric shook his head angrily, his hands balled into fists. He smashed a hole in the wall, then recited the list of those who got silverized. The honored dead. Warhead, Roswell, the Tank . . . eight in all.

"So there's still fourteen left," I said.

Cedric smiled in spite of his anger. "Fifteen," he said. "Tonight, you get made—and you'll be a full-fledged werewolf."

I suppressed a shiver. "Just what I've always wanted."

"I know."

"What about Marvin? What happened to him?"

Cedric's face went red. I thought he might punch another hole in the wall. "That low-life stinking traitor knows better than to show his ugly face around here again. His sister joins the wolf hunters, and he saves her, instead of fighting for us. Don't you worry, Red—we'll find Marvin, and when we do, he's gonna suffer for what he did last night." Cedric took a deep breath, releasing his anger with it.

I thought back to the fight the night before, and how it ended. If I was on Cedric's good side, maybe I could ask about it.

"Cedric—I saw something strange last night. Even stranger than a pack of werewolves, I mean. Whatever it was, it flew over my head."

"We'll talk about that later," he said. "You deserve to know, and so you will know."

Then Cedric clamped his hand down on my shoulder like a brother. "Last night I learned who my true friends are." He grabbed my hand and pressed a set of keys into them. "You did good, Red. You take your car back—it don't matter if your grandma sees you riding around in it now, since she already knows you're on our side. And if there's anything else you want, all you gotta do is ask."

I couldn't believe my luck. In one minute I went from being werewolf chow to being a decorated hero. I was behind the wheel of my car again, and I was so tempted to take off and leave all of this behind. The car was full of gas, and I had good reason to leave . . . but that meant I was leaving Marissa and Grandma at the mercy of the Wolves. Or was it the Wolves being left at their mercy? After all, they had taken out eight of them without my help, making the Wolves think there were dozens of hunters on their tail.

But running away was something I had never done. It just

wasn't in me. In the end, I drove around town until I had the feel of my Mustang again. Driving around town gave me a little bit of comfort. A sense of my territory. Then I went to the Wolves' new hangout, which Cedric had told me about. It was one Grandma didn't know about, and I'm sure the Wolves weren't too happy about its location, because it was beyond Abject End Park, smack in the heart of the Canyons. Apparently we had permission from the Crypts to be there, thanks to my little mission of diplomacy last week.

Dead storehouses and factories loomed above me, as they had the last time I ventured into the Canyons, but this time I had wheels. Cedric had claimed an extinct dance club as our new hangout. Dust covered a wooden dance floor. A disco ball still hung at its center. Chairs and tables were stacked and pushed to the side. Some tables still had salt-and-pepper shakers, left exactly as they had been the day the club closed, probably long before I born.

"We'll lick our wounds, and we'll go out again tonight," Cedric told us. "We'll do it in spite of the hunters." And then he said, "I want them to know they've failed."

The others all sat in groups, some still sleeping off the night, others reliving the worst of it. Through all of this, Loogie sat off in the corner by himself, not talking, not wanting to be near any of us. He watched. Not just watched, but leered. I could feel his eyes like they were drilling holes in everyone he looked at, as if he was looking at the world through a new, more intense set of eyes.

I went over to him and sat down next to him. He didn't say anything for a while.

"Freaky," he finally said. Nothing else. Just "Freaky."

"What's freaky?"

"Everything," he said. I noticed that he looked even paler than he had the day before. I wondered if there was some werewolf sickness going around that I didn't know about. His skin was downright pasty. Almost green.

"Where's Cedric?"

"Negotiating," was all he said.

I turned away from him for just a second, and when I turned back, he wasn't there anymore. Instead, he was sitting on the other side of me.

"What the . . ."

"See, didn't I tell you? Freaky."

A/C came to sit down next to us. "Man, Loogie, you got that Bobby Tanaka look." At the mention of Bobby Tanaka, a couple of the other guys came over.

Loogie gave a bitter laugh. "Oh, I guess you could say that."

I glanced around, and no one was saying anything. No one could even look at one another. "What happened to Bobby Tanaka, anyway?" I asked. "And don't give me that 'some things are worse than death' line, because I don't buy it."

No one would talk.

"I don't know," said Moxie.

"Me neither," said El Toro. "It happened before most of us became Wolves."

"*I* know," said Loogie.

All eyes turned to him.

"Don't talk about it," said A/C. "Cedric hates when anyone talks about it."

Loogie shrugged, not caring. "But Cedric's not here, is he? And even if he was, not even he can stop me now."

By this point most of the remaining Wolves had pulled up chairs. It was like Loogie's presence was a black hole in the room, drawing everyone to him. I wondered if it was just my imagination.

"It happened a couple of years ago, when the Wolves were just starting out," Loogie began. "There were about ten of us then. Cedric didn't like the idea that there was another gang in town almost as powerful as us. He was just as power hungry then as he is now. He decided we should make the Canyons our territory, too, and take on the Crypts. So one full moon, already in werewolf form, we stormed into the Canyons. But the farther down the abandoned old streets we got, the denser the fog got. It wasn't a normal fog. It was thick and stunk like swamp rot. It wasn't a city smell—it was unnatural, like the whole place was built on rotting dirt from some other dark, faraway place." Loogie turned to me. "A stench like that is unbearable to a werewolf," he explained. "We got supersensitive noses. Anyway, the smell was so strong it made us howl in agony. That's when they came. Dropping down from the ledges of the old burned-out factories."

"The Crypts?" Moxie asked.

"Bats. Dozens of bats, swarming us, clawing at us, screeching in our ears, but no matter how fast we moved to swat them away, they were faster. In the end, they attacked one of us, and only one. A dozen of them bit into Bobby Tanaka. Why they chose him, I don't know. They could have gone after any of us, but he was just the unlucky one."

By now everyone in the room was listening to him. I was so drawn into Loogie's tale, I couldn't look away.

"If you think nothing can scare a werewolf, you're wrong, because when one of those bats turned into a girl—you've never heard wolf howls so loud. It was Rowena, the Crypts' leader. She just stood there, smiling at us as the bats behind her drained every last bit of Bobby Tanaka's blood in a minute flat. Then Rowena turned back into a bat herself and flew off with the rest of them."

"Wow," was all I could say.

"That's not the worst of it," said A/C, picking up the story. "The Crypts drained his blood and left him there wailing in agony, because, see, he was a werewolf—he couldn't die . . . But to be alive without any blood left inside you . . . it was horrible. He said it felt like someone had sliced open his gut and sewn it full of stones."

Some of the other Wolves reached down to their own stomachs and held them, as if they could feel a gut full of stones themselves.

"It went on like that for two days," A/C said, "with Bobby screaming in pain, until Cedric finally silverized him, to put him out of his misery. We all knew the Crypts had done it as a warning. *'Mess with us, and you'll all end up like Bobby.'* So we never messed with them again."

"Until now," said Loogie, and pulled down the collar of his shirt to show two little puncture marks on his neck. Everyone gasped.

"So how come you're not screaming, Loogie?" asked one of

the others. "If the Crypts got you, how come you didn't end up like Bobby?"

"Vampires got a choice," Loogie said. "Just like we do. We can eat our prey, or we can just bite 'em, and turn them into a werewolf." Then Loogie pulled down the collar of his shirt a little farther to show two more bites, just beneath the first. "Three bites over three nights and poof! You're a vampire, too."

The room was silent, until I spoke. "So . . . it was *you* I saw last night. That flying fox!"

"No way."

"That's crazy!"

"You're joking, Loogie, right?"

Loogie shook his head. "Want me to 'wing' right here in front of you? That's what they call turning into a bat—'winging.'"

But no one wanted to see it. We believed.

"So, Loogie," asked A/C, "are you a werewolf now, or a vampire?"

"He's both," said Cedric. We turned to see him standing behind us. "He's what the Mexicans call a *chupacabra*. The strength of a werewolf, the power of a vampire, able to change at will and fly all night long."

The Wolves looked at Cedric in amazement.

"How come Loogie gets to fly?" asked A/C. "Why not me?"

"Yeah, why not us?" complained the others.

"Don't worry," said Cedric. "I've been working things out with the Crypts. Thanks to a new pact between them and us, in a few days we're all going to be just like Loogie."

18

▲

"WHICH SIDE ARE YOU ON?"

What do you do if you're a kid living in Pearl Harbor, and you just happen to pick up a message on your walkie-talkie that the Japanese are going to be attacking tomorrow? What if those same Japanese pilots had taken you in and made you their friend?

I had this massive bit of knowledge that no one else knew. Cedric was building himself an army—not just werewolves, but *vampire* werewolves! I mean, how do you kill a vampire werewolf? A silver stake through the heart? What would happen if Cedric got his way, and he started sending the surviving pack members to distant cities, with the power of flight, and a hunger not only for flesh, but for blood? The whole pack was excited about the thought, thrilled by it . . . and the thing is, so was I. As much as I wanted to stop it before it started, I wanted to fly like Loogie did. I wanted to know the hunger, and the feeling of satisfying it.

Back in my car, I drove aimlessly, breaking all the rules I had learned in Driver's Ed. Finally, exhausted beyond belief, I pulled over in a parking lot, leaned my head against the wheel, and closed my eyes, trying to sort out my thoughts. Good and evil, right and wrong, had all blended into a murky gray haze.

The next thing I remember, I was turning down Forest Boulevard and parking out in front of Grandma's. I didn't know what I would tell her, but I felt sure I would have the words once I found her.

Her door was unlocked. That wasn't a good sign. Carefully I went in. "Grandma?"

I felt that strange surge of déjà vu—this was exactly as it had been on the day Cedric lay hidden in her bed and stole that bag of blood money.

"Grandma?"

I pushed open the door to her room. This time no one was in the bed—not Grandma, not Cedric, nobody.

"Grandma, are you here? We have to talk. It's important!"

It was getting dark very quickly. Night was falling like a curtain over the day, or maybe it was just the dense trees outside. On Grandma's nightstand sat a glass, and in that glass sat her gross old dentures, all magnified by the water inside. Then a shaft of light pierced a slit in the curtains. It was the moon. It was already night, and the full moon was rising! The moonlight hit the glass, and right before my eyes, the teeth in that glass began to change. They stretched and grew, the canines elongating, getting sharp, and growing until the horrible dentures were so big, they broke the glass.

I couldn't scream, I couldn't breathe, then the bathroom door slammed open, and out loped a werewolf, with big, frizzy gray fur and old familiar eyes.

"Been waiting for you, Red," the Grandma-wolf said. "Glad you came by." She picked up the wolf chompers lying on the table and stuck them into her toothless, wolfen mouth.

"There we are," she said, baring her teeth. "The better to eat you with!"

She lunged at me, I screamed, and *wham*—

—I bumped my head on the steering wheel of my Mustang.

I jumped, still reeling, still believing that the dream was real. It took a few good minutes for me to convince myself that I was still there, in the parking lot, at the wheel of my Mustang, and not at Grandma's house.

As I caught my breath, and shook off the evil feel of the nightmare, I realized that part of the dream was real. The part about the moon . . . because it was night, the full moon was on the rise, and I could already hear the far-off howls of wolves on the prowl.

The battery on my watch had died, so I had no idea what time it was, but time didn't matter to me anymore—not in the normal sense. All that mattered was that the moon was full, and it was night, which meant that every second was an eternity, and dawn was a lifetime away.

The howls echoed from the faces of buildings, making it hard to tell which direction they came from, and as I drove, turning corner after corner, I felt like I was chasing my own tail. And then I thought, *Pretty soon, I* will *have a tail, if Cedric bites me.* The thought was so powerful, it took my mind off the road, and before I knew what was happening, I barreled through a red light, and a Mercedes came flying out of the intersection, right into my path.

I slammed on the brakes and cranked the wheel to the right. A horn blared, and I missed the Mercedes by inches, but I was still careening out of control. I hit the curb, pedestrians scattered, and I plowed over an empty bus-stop bench.

No! No, not now! I can't have an accident now!

If this morning had blessed me with good luck, tonight was cursing me with bad. I threw the car into reverse, but the wheels just spun. I put it into drive, but that didn't help either. I hopped out of the car to see green radiator fluid pouring out, and the broken bench wedged under the car in such a way that only one of the four wheels was actually touching the ground.

My car! My beautiful car!

But no, I couldn't worry about the car now. Was that a distant scream I heard? A woman attacked by a wolf? Was it just my imagination?

"You all right, son?" said an old man from the group of gawking pedestrians.

"Get out of the streets!" I told them all. "Get to your homes before it's too late!" But they just stared at me like I was insane. Nothing I could do would convince them of the danger. Now, with my car useless, I took off on foot.

I ran till I was out of breath, and further, to the very end of my endurance. Sweat poured from me like rain, and a heaviness filled my lungs. My head began to spin, but I had to push myself on. I heard another howl, not so distant this time. A snarl—it could have been around the next corner. I had lost track of where I was, and realized I had no weapon—even if I found the Wolves, what could I do? Talk them out of devouring innocent people? As if they would actually listen. It's what werewolves did—it's what they were. Predators. The only way to stop a predator was to cage it or kill it, and I don't think there were any bars in the world strong enough to cage in Cedric and his gang.

If you can't beat them, join them, said a nagging voice in my head. *It's what they want. It's what you want. Don't deny it!*

I put my hands against my head, trying to press the voice away, but it was too deep in me now. *It's out of your hands,* the voice said. *Let nature take its course. And accept your true nature. You're one of them. You've been one of them since the moment you stepped into Troll Bridge Hollow.*

Then, out of nowhere, something huge, hairy, and reeking like a zoo pounced and brought me down hard. I hit my head on the pavement. Massive paws pressed down on my shoulders, pinning me to the ground, and all I could see was a fang-filled mouth set in a wide-open snarl. My whole head could have fit in that mouth.

I knew who this was. I knew from the single gold fang, dripping werewolf saliva.

"Which side are you on?" said the familiar voice of a girl, from behind Marvin.

"Marissa! Thank God you're—" The Marvin-wolf snarled in my face. It was a deep, jagged roar—an awful sound, like the voice of a demon. I tried to see where Marissa was, but the Marvin-beast filled my entire view.

"Answer me!" Marissa demanded. "And if Marvin smells that you're lying, he'll swallow you whole!"

I believed he could. That horrible mouth. Those awful teeth. And I also believed that he could smell a lie.

"I . . . I . . ."

Marvin's claws began to dig into my shoulder.

"The truth!" Marissa said.

"I . . . I don't know," I told her. "I don't know which side I'm on." I had no choice but to admit it now.

It wasn't the answer either of them was expecting, but it must have smelled true, because the pressure on my shoulder eased. Marvin backed off of me. Finally I could see Marissa behind him, standing on the cracked sidewalk of the dimly lit street.

"You can't be on two sides at once," she said. "Choose, or get out of the way."

I looked at snarling Marvin, then I looked back to her. "How about you?" I asked. "Which side are you on?"

She didn't answer me right away. "You were right all along about Marvin," she said. "He's been a full-fledged Wolf for a month, but I didn't know until last night." She looked at him lovingly, and gently brushed a thick lock of fur back from his eyes. "He became a Wolf to save our family."

"I don't understand."

"Wolves won't attack other Wolves' families. They're the only ones in town who are safe. So Marvin became one of them. He sacrificed himself to save me and our parents."

"You weren't off-limits last night."

She grinned. "I attacked first. All bets were off. But Marvin here protected me."

Marvin let out a gentle purr. It had never occurred to me that Marvin might have a reason to be a Wolf beyond his own selfish ambition. Now I understood why he hated me so much.

He had ensured Marissa's safety by becoming a Wolf—the last thing he wanted was to see her dating a Wolf-in-training.

"Marvin turned on the pack last night, by saving me," she said. "Now he has no choice but to fight against Cedric, too." Only then did I see that Marissa held the crossbow to her side.

"Grandma! Where is she? Is she all right?"

Suddenly Marvin turned his head, hearing something I couldn't hear.

"They're coming!" Marissa said. "Run, Marvin!"

Marvin glared at me—the same glare I'd seen when his eyes were human. Grandma was right; there was something about the eyes that never changed. Then he bounded off with the speed of a cheetah: a brown blur down a dark street, gone in an instant.

Marissa ducked into a doorway, disappearing into the shadows. "So you were right about Marvin being a werewolf," she said from the darkness. "But you were wrong about him being bad."

The air around us became silent. Too silent, like the moment before a storm. "Better hide, and hope we're downwind," Marissa said.

But I didn't hide. I stood there, out in the open, and watched the wolf pack come around the corner. They were all there, bounding headlong on all fours, like racehorses, with Cedric in the lead and Loogie winging just a few feet above. They saw me right away and came to a halt. I had no idea what they were going to do.

"I know you're after Marvin," I said. "With all of you on it, you're sure to catch him." *Yeah,* I thought, *and with all of you on it, no one else in town will get eaten by werewolves tonight.* I wondered if Marissa had thought of that, too.

Cedric couldn't speak in wolf form, but his body language was easy to read. A quick gesture of his head called me over to him. I stepped from the curb, and then Cedric Soames, the cold, callous leader of the Wolves, knelt down. He wanted me to climb on his back and ride with them. So I did.

Suddenly something grazed past my ear and struck a werewolf to my right. A roar of pain, the wolf turned, and I could see sudden shock and agony in its green eyes. *A/C has green eyes,* I thought. *That wolf is A/C!* Suddenly he collapsed to the ground, writhing in pain. A silver-tipped crossbow arrow had pierced his flank.

A second arrow whizzed out of the darkness, nailing a mailbox across the street. Cedric roared and took off. I gripped his fur to keep from falling. The rest of the wolves followed, and before long we were racing at full speed, ignoring the shooter, following Marvin's scent instead of Marissa's. I turned back only once to see A/C roar, squirm in pain, then go limp.

Which side was I on? There was no time to search for answers. All I could do now was ride on a werewolf's back, toward a destiny as hidden as the dark side of a full moon.

19
▲
A GUT FULL OF STONES

Marvin stayed one step ahead of us, weaving in and out of the city for what seemed like hours. Several times the pack broke up and tried to circle around him, but just as he had weaved his way down the football field when he was Marvelous Marvin, star running back, he kept just out of the pack's reach. This chase was a waste of the pack's time. I knew it, and most of the pack must have known it, but I wasn't going to lean over and whisper into Cedric's ear. Every minute the pack was forced to follow Marvin was another minute they weren't "wolfing." Whether he intended to or not, Marvin Flowers saved a whole lot of lives that night.

As I rode Cedric, like the lead man in a posse, I began to feel a strange sense of power. *You could lead this group,* that mischievous voice in my head kept telling me. *Consigliere?* Sure, maybe for a while, but then there was Denver. I had already claimed the Mile High City as my own. In a few years' time, I could be there, handpicking my own pack. This night's wild ride through the moonlit city was just a taste of what it could be like. Then I looked up at Loogie, flitting back and forth above us. The possibilities were endless.

As dawn approached, it seemed that Marvin was finally getting tired. The pack wasn't just following his scent anymore, now they could see him. Even I, with my limited human vision, could see him loping steadily in front of us, crossing through the mist of a lonely, run-down park. I recognized it right away. It was Abject End Park, gateway to the Canyons. Marvin was leading us back to our new lair. Maybe he knew it was over for him, and he wanted to end it there. Or maybe he had something else in mind.

We reached the old dance club. The dense mist of the Canyons poured in through the door. Cedric stalked in first with the pack close behind. I hopped off Cedric's back. There was something wrong in here, but I wasn't quite sure what it was. It was something I had caught out of the corner of my eye, but I hadn't seen it long enough for it to leave an impression on my brain.

"Marvin, we know you're in here," I said. Cedric growled in a fury. I put up my hand to calm him down. "Let me handle this for you," I told Cedric. "I promise you won't be disappointed."

Cedric snarled at me again, then watched to see what I would do. The whole pack kept their eyes on me as I stepped out into the middle of the old dance floor. I had to be referee here. Maybe, if I played this right, everyone could get what they wanted. But then, how could that be, when all Cedric wanted was to see Marvin dead?

"Let's make a deal, Marvin." I had no idea what the deal could possibly be, but I knew if I kept talking, it would keep Cedric and the pack from tearing the place apart looking for Marvin so they could tear him apart. "A deal, Marvin. A really good deal." Why I wanted to save Marvin, I had no idea. He had done nothing but make life miserable for me since that day he washed my windshield. "Cedric and the pack will let you live, in return for something," I said.

Cedric's eyes narrowed, and he bared his teeth at me. *This had better be good,* the look said.

"Something in return," I said again, stalling. And then it came to me! "Cedric will let you live . . . but someday, he will ask you to do a favor for him. And whatever that favor is, you can't refuse." I glanced to Cedric, and that angry wolf gaze changed into a coyote grin, because what I offered Marvin had come straight out of one of Cedric's beloved Mafia movies!

We waited, and after a few moments Marvin came slinking out of the shadows, onto the dance floor. The pack surrounded him, and Cedric went back to growling, just in case Marvin had forgotten how furious he was.

Then the feeling fell upon me again. Something here didn't look right. As the pack formed a growling circle around Marvin, and as Marvin crouched and crawled on his belly like a naughty dog, I tried to retrace all the things I had seen over the past few seconds that could have given me that freaky feeling. I glanced at the door: still partway open, with mist spilling in. I looked down to the dance floor, now scuffed and scratched by werewolf claws. I lifted my eyes up to the old disco ball, swinging slightly up above, all sharp and pointy.

Sharp and pointy?

I glanced up again. That was no disco ball! I wasn't quite sure what it was at first. It looked like a ball of gray clay, with silverware sticking out of it in all directions. Forks, knives, spoons. *Silver* ware.

Then I realized that the ball of clay in the middle might not be clay at all. It might just be plastic explosive.

A wire stretched from the little ball across the ceiling to a far wall. Leaving the dance floor, I followed the path of the wire to an old DJ booth, where I saw none other than my own little old grandma, dressed in black like a special-ops agent, clutching a detonator.

She snapped her head to see me at the threshold, and her jaw dropped. She was scared. Scared of me—scared that I would give her away to the wolves. I turned to look at them. They were all on the dance floor, going up to Marvin, one by one swatting him with their paws, like some sort of wolfen punishment ritual.

Grandma, her hand shaking, lowered a finger toward the red button on the detonator. But I grabbed her hand before she could touch it.

"You'll have to kill me to stop me, Red," she whispered. "Because it's either me, or them."

Still I held her hand. "No, Grandma, no. Not this way!"

"What way, then? There's only one way with werewolves: kill or be killed."

"No," I said. "Let me think!"

I turned again to the wolves. They were so wrapped up in their punishment of Marvin, they had no idea that death hung right above their heads. Marvin was in on this! He had to be. He was sent racing through the city all night to keep the wolves busy while Grandma, and Marissa, set up the deadly silverware bomb.

"Let me think, Grandma!" Fourteen Wolves remained today. Fifteen if I took the bite. Packs would be sprouting up in one city, then another, then another. Including Denver. I pulled the detonator from her.

"Red, no!"

I could be a leader. I could rule a city by night.

"Do the right thing, Red."

I could fly on the wings of a bat—undying and undead at the same time!

"There's only one right thing! You know it in your heart!"

My life and my future hinged on the choice that I made. I knew what I *should* do, I knew what I *wanted* to do. . . .

"No more thinking, Red. Choose!"

I could have a life as a supernatural creature of the dark. It was a fine fantasy, except for one thing. Werewolves were merciless killers that lived on human flesh.

"Choose now!"

I screamed with the agony of my choice and brought my finger down on the red button.

The explosion blew out the glass of the DJ booth. It blew the chairs and tables across the room. Forks, knives, and even spoons were embedded half an inch deep into the walls, and when I looked at the dance floor, I saw a dozen wolves dancing. They spun, they rolled, they howled, pulling the silverware out of their wounds, but it would do no good. It was too late, the deadly silver had already worked its way through their veins. Wounded and wailing, they spun, they crawled, they shivered, and they died. My enemies. My friends. The wolves died, and my tears stung so badly, I wanted to rip my eyes right out of their sockets. How dare I cry for them? How dare I care enough to cry?

Two more wolves came bounding out from beneath tables. Two that hadn't been caught by the explosion of silverware, and then there was Loogie, flapping wildly across the rafters above, not sure what to do, turning to wolf, to bat, and back to wolf again. Marissa popped out behind a pole, a quiver of silver-tipped arrows at her side. She loaded them into the crossbow.

"Over there," I said through my tears. "By the back door!"

Marissa turned and fired, her arrow lodging in Klutz's flank. He fell and wailed as the silver did its deadly damage.

"The window!" El Toro leaped out the window, and Marissa and I followed right behind. He was already disappearing into the mist.

"I can't see him," said Marissa.

"I can!" I took the crossbow from her, took aim at the fading figure, and fired. I couldn't see him anymore, but the wail and the thud as he fell to the ground told me all I needed to know. In a moment, all was silent. A dim blue light had begun to fill the darkness. The coming dawn.

"What about Marvin?" I asked Marissa.

She shook her head, her eyes filling with tears. "He went onto that dance floor to draw the wolves there. He sacrificed himself to save me."

"I'm sorry."

"Red—look!" I turned to see the mist before us begin to swirl, and a snout appeared, followed by a pair of eyes that were accusing, and angrier than I had ever seen them before.

It was Cedric.

I raised the crossbow. "Run!" I said to Marissa.

"No," she said. "We'll face him together."

Cedric stood there, breathing his anger in short, ferocious breaths. I put my finger on the trigger. I began to pull back . . . and then I stopped.

Cedric didn't attack. He didn't lunge for me; he just stood there. He was daring me.

Kill me, you coward, that look said. *Kill me, you traitor. You liar. You double-crossing false friend. Shoot me between the eyes. I dare you.*

I couldn't do it. I couldn't pull that trigger. And he knew it.

That's when he lunged, his mouth wide, teeth bared. Marissa screamed, tugging me back. I pulled the trigger, but the arrow flew uselessly up to the sky—and suddenly I was surrounded in a flutter of black.

Wings brushed passed me, dozens upon dozens, heading straight for Cedric. Cedric roared, and in a second he had forgotten about me, because he was covered by countless bats, every one of them digging their fangs into his wolf flesh, sucking deep, draining.

They were done in less than a minute. Then they fluttered away as quickly as they had come, leaving Cedric's wolfen form in a heap on the ground, moaning. His fur was already growing shorter. His snout pushed in to become a human jaw. The mist around us was glowing a brighter blue with each passing second. Dawn had arrived.

In a moment Cedric's transformation was complete. He was in human form again, and the bites from the vampire bats covered his body like measles. He gasped over and over again, like he couldn't get enough air. His eyes rolled in his head. I went over to him, kneeling down.

"No blood!" he said. "No blood! Bobby Tanaka! No blood!"

They had drained his blood, and there was nothing I could do. I took off my jacket and covered him, and Marissa, for all her hatred of him, took off hers as well. I rolled it up and put it behind his head as a pillow.

"Horrible!" he gasped. "Pain." He clutched his gut. "Like stones in my stomach."

I couldn't imagine the feeling. "It's okay," I said. "It's okay." But I knew it wasn't. It would never be okay.

Cedric tried to hold back his pain and looked at me with anguish in his eyes. "Why?" he said. "Why did you? Why did you, Red?"

"You said werewolves were a part of nature," I told him. "And maybe you're right. But it's also part of nature for humans to protect themselves. That's why, Cedric."

He closed his eyes, either from the pain of the vampire bites, or maybe from the pain of my betrayal. Then he opened them again. "Mother Nature's a tough old witch," Cedric gasped out. "Like your grandma."

I could feel his heart beating, but with nothing to pump, it just pounded against itself.

"Finish it," Cedric said. "Please, finish it."

I knew what he wanted, but the silver had all been spent. No more arrows, nothing. And then I realized that there was some silver left. *Keep it close to your heart,* Mom had told me. I did, and I guess it protected me. I reached into my shirt and pulled out the little coin with the image of Saint Gabriel. I took it from around my neck and gently lifted Cedric's hand. There were bat bites all over his palm, little bloodless wounds. I took the coin and pressed it into his palm, closing his fingers around it.

"I hope this pays the fare, Cedric," I said gently, "to wherever you're going."

He gripped the coin tightly, making sure the silver touched the open wounds on his hands, and he closed his eyes. He shuddered once, shuddered again, and then he was gone.

I stared at him long after he was dead, and when I finally looked up, a beautiful girl in a flowing black gown stood before me.

"Hello, Red. Sorry it had to end like this, but what kind of babysitter would I be if I let Cedric get you?"

Grandma and Marissa came up behind me. "Who in blazes is that?" Grandma asked.

"Rowena," I told her. "Queen of the Crypts."

Out of the mist behind her stepped Loogie, in human form. Well, sort of human, considering his recent undead status.

"We missed one!" said Grandma.

Rowena put up her hand. "Don't worry about him," she said gently. "He's one of us now. We'll keep him out of trouble."

Loogie looked at Cedric's body and lowered his head in respect.

"Go home," Rowena told us. "My girls will clean up the mess."

"We have to count the bodies," I told her. "To make sure we got them all."

Then Rowena came over to me and whispered into my ear. "You'll never get them all," she said. "They're werewolves, and no matter how many you kill, there will always be one more."

The thought made me shiver, but I knew it was true. Grandma got all of Xavier's gang, and still the wolves came back. Even if we got all of Cedric's, it didn't mean we were safe forever.

"The Wolves all had families," Rowena reminded me. "They won't take kindly to what happened here tonight—and who knows if there's a baby brother or sister who took the bite. So my advice to you, Red, is to fix that car of yours, and make sure it's faster than anyone can run—man, or wolf."

She backed away. I nodded to her in understanding, then she and Loogie turned into bats and flew deep into the Canyons.

"Hmm," said Grandma. "Vampires, huh?"

"Yeah."

"Somebody else's problem." She turned and walked away.

I took one more look at Cedric, the immortal leader of the pack, not so immortal after all. Then Marissa gently grabbed my arm, to lead me away. As dawn broke over the city, we walked out of that dismal place, across Abject End Park, and headed for home.

20

▲

THE BETTER TO
WATCH YOU WITH

I've been watching the news," I told Marissa the next day in the antique shop. "There aren't any reports of a gang war, or anything. It's like it never happened."

Marissa organized a shelf of knickknacks, not looking at me much. "I guess the Crypts cleaned up real good," she said. She glanced at me once, then looked away. "I did see one report, though," she told me. "They were talking about a pack of stray dogs roaming the streets. Animal Control is on it, but they haven't found anything."

"I guess they never will," I said. Then I reached over and took her hand. "I'm sorry about Marvin."

She tried to force a smile. "My parents think he ran off to Hollywood, like he always threatened to—and don't you tell them any different."

I'm sure her parents knew the truth, though, or at least some of it. I could see it in their eyes when they came by to pick up Marissa that afternoon. There are just some things parents know about you. Like whether or not you're a werewolf.

As for my parents, when they came back from their trip, they knew something had happened to me while they were gone, they just weren't sure what it was. "You're growing up, Red," was the closest my father came to putting his finger on it. The way they looked at me freaked me out so much, I gave myself the silver test—we all did, Grandma, Marissa, and me, gripping a silver spoon tightly in our hands—making sure it was silver and not just stainless steel. No reaction. It was the last time the three of us met together as a team of werewolf hunters.

With my car in the shop, I did a lot of walking over the next few weeks, just to listen to the gossip in the neighborhood. According to the rumors, the Wolves just disappeared, as they had twenty years ago. Some people thought they just left to find a better town to terrorize. "Good riddance to bad rubbish," they would say. There was, of course, a story being whispered about a single, hairy creature descending from the skies during the next full moon, draining all the blood from a couple of vicious junkyard dogs, but no one really believed it. Aside from that, the neighborhood was soon back to normal, short a handful of troublemakers that no one was going to miss.

There were some people out there who knew the truth, though. I know this because of all the envelopes that kept showing up in my mailbox and under my door. Thank-you notes, packed with money. Secret payments from relieved citizens, just like the ones Grandma had gotten years ago. It turns out she and Marissa were now getting those envelopes, too.

"Ain't no shame in accepting payment for services rendered," Grandma said. I put mine in the safe, where Grandma's first batch of blood money had hidden all those years. "Summer job," I told my parents, and although they usually asked me a million questions, this time they knew enough not to.

Rowena was right about one thing. Every now and again, I would catch nasty, evil looks from people who had a son or a brother in the Wolves. Maybe they were just normal human beings, hating me for taking away their loved one, but then again you never know for sure what's boiling in a person's blood. But as long as my Mustang is in top shape, I don't need to worry. I can outrun anything.

Anything, that is, but the memory of Cedric Soames.

It took me a month to dredge up the nerve to walk down Cedric's street. I half expected to see his ghost in the shadows of the alleys, but instead, all I saw was his sister, Tina, playing hopscotch with her friends out front. She stopped for a moment when she saw me, then continued her game.

"My mama says Cedric got himself a good job, far away, and he ain't gonna be back no more," Tina said.

"If that's what your mama says, I guess it's true."

"I don't believe it, though," Tina said.

"So where do you think he is?"

Tina hopped four times, picked up the little beanbag, and went back to the first square. "I think he got himself arrested for all that bad stuff he does. I think he's locked away in a dark, dark place." And then she left the little chalk squares of her game and came right up to me. "I'll tell you this, though," she said, staring me in the eye like a devil child. "There ain't no place in this world or the next that can hold Cedric in. He'll come back, Red, you wait and see. And when he does, those who crossed him are gonna pay."

As she went back to her game, I swore to myself I would never go down Cedric's street again.

It didn't make a difference, though, because Tina turned out to be right. One year after the Wolves fell, Cedric came back.

My parents weren't off sailing in the Mediterranean this time, but they were out for the evening. I came home to an empty house, or so I thought. I didn't think there was anything significant about the day. I mean, there are some days that just burn themselves into your mental calendar. August 4 was that date for me, Marissa, and Grandma. That was the day the Wolves fell, but that anniversary had already come and gone without any fireworks.

What I didn't consider was that the lunar calendar doesn't quite track along with the months. The date was August 9. The second full moon of summer. I had gotten a summer job taking old junkyard cars and restoring them, so was pretty dirty when I got home. I figured I'd clean up, then call Marissa, to see if she wanted to go out for a burger or something. I went into my bedroom, half lit by the fading twilight. That's when I saw him.

I was so surprised I let out a quaking groan of fear—not a scream, because your first reaction is never a scream. The scream comes later, when your mind has a chance to catch up with your gut, and you know what you're dealing with.

He was there, in the corner of the room, watching me.

I got my balance back, took a deep breath, and slowly approached.

There on my bookshelf sat a skull. I didn't recognize it at first, until I took a good look at the teeth and imagined what a pair of lips might look like in front of them. Grinning. Scowling. There was no doubt. This was the skull of Cedric Soames.

Grandma had told me that werewolf flesh turns to dust much faster than human flesh, but she had also told me that their bones last an eternity. "Hard as diamonds those bones are," she had said, "which means the earth can never quite be free of a werewolf."

How the skull got here, I didn't know. I thought that maybe his creepy little sister, Tina, had broken in and set it on my shelf to freak me out. Or maybe Loogie had flown it in on bat wings, to make sure I never forgot. But the Soames family had moved clear across the country a few months after Cedric disappeared. And as for Loogie . . . well, everyone knows a vampire can't enter someone's house without being invited.

As I stood there, my heart beating in overdrive, the last of the twilight faded, and the skull on my shelf transformed into the skull of a wolf.

Grandma and Marissa came over that night. We all sat on my bed and stared at the werewolf skull, which just stared back at us, unblinking, its fangs glistening with some kind of strange ectoplasm, like supernatural saliva.

"What's it doing here, Grandma?" I asked. "What does it want?"

Grandma just shook her head. "I know an awful lot about werewolves, Red, but don't know everything. Could be that

Cedric was just too powerful to die outright. Could be some part of him is trying to come back."

"Why me?" I asked, but I already knew the answer. I was his *consigliere*. And I was the one who betrayed him.

The skull vanished when the moon began to wane, but appeared again at the next full moon, and it has been coming back ever since. I've grown used to it now. Well, maybe not used to it, but resigned to it, like a death-row inmate is resigned to his fate. Because, you see, when I wake up in the morning, always just before dawn, that werewolf skull is closer to my bed that it had been when I went to sleep. Each month it gets closer, no matter where I set it before I go to sleep. I don't fear it will devour me, but I do know this: One day I'll wake up to find it clamped down on my arm, breaking just enough skin to pass down the curse.

But that hasn't happened yet, so for now I wait, looking deep into those hollow eye sockets, whispering to it so only he and I can hear.

"My, my, Cedric, what dark, empty eyes you have."

"The better to watch you with, Red . . . The better to watch you with . . ."

Turn the page for a preview of the next
darkfusion novel,

1

TO THE BONE

I will always remember the lights, stark and hot, shining on me from every angle. They exposed my face for the whole world to see. Being onstage in front of hundreds of people should have been a high point of my life, but those lights . . . I felt naked beneath them. My pores had opened—I could feel sweat running down my face, coursing around zits and moles like boulders in a river, then pouring down my neck, to soak the collar of my blouse. I knew even before we began that things were going to go wrong.

"Contestant number thirteen," the head judge said, his voice booming into the microphone. "Cara DeFido."

I stood up. There were hundreds of people in the audience. I couldn't see them, but I did hear whispers. I tried to make myself believe they weren't whispering about me.

"Spell the word *unprepossessing*."

That's an easy one, I thought. There was a little tittering from certain members of the audience when he said the word, but I didn't let it get to me.

"Unprepossessing." I said. "*U-N-P-R-E-P-O-S-S-E-S-S-I-N-G*. Unprepossessing."

"That's correct."

There was some halfhearted applause as I sat back down.

Everyone's good at something. I can spell. I guess it's just an inborn ability—something to do with the way my brain is wired. It's the kind of skill that goes unnoticed except at spelling bees. Kids can win thousands of dollars at the national level. "There's a market for every skill," my dad says, "even the weird ones." So once a year I get to go up onstage for the county spelling bee, and I always win it. I never go on to the state or national spelling bees, though. I could, but I don't. Those bigger contests are televised; I got my reasons for not getting in front of cameras.

As I sat there and waited for my next turn, the word I had just spelled stuck in my throat like a pill, just dissolving there, tasting bitter.

Unprepossessing.

It was another one of those nice words for "ugly." Even nicer than *plain*. It was just a coincidence that the judge's computer came up with that word for me to spell, but still it bothered me. Momma would have called it ironic. The Almighty showing He's got Himself a sense of humor. I'm sure that's what she was thinking out there in the audience.

Well, she's not me. The contests she went out for when she was my age were beauty contests, not spelling bees. She was possessing, *pre*possessing—there was no "un" about it.

"Contestant thirteen," the judge's voice boomed.

In the previous round, there had been five more eliminations. Only six of us remained. I stood up and felt the searing spotlight on me again.

The judge looked at the word that had been thrown up on his

computer screen, and he hesitated. He glanced at the judge next to him, who only shrugged. He took a deep breath and turned to me.

"Please spell *abomination*."

Some gasps of surprise from the audience. A few snickers.

The heat I felt in my ears, then cheeks had nothing to do with the lights. I knew I was going blotchy red. I tried to tell myself it was just coincidence again, but deep down I knew it wasn't. This word was too easy. The other kids were getting words like *cairn-gorm* and *pneumonectomy*. Whether this was the Almighty having a major laugh or something other, I couldn't figure out yet.

"Abomination," I said. "*A-B-O-M-I-N-A-T-I-O-N*. Abomination."

"Correct."

I sat back down and looked at the crack-nail toes sticking through the tips of my sandals.

There's that old joke: "Beauty is only skin deep, but ugly goes right to the bone." But they're wrong—because with me it goes deeper than the bone. It goes right to the marrow. I once overheard our pastor say to one of the other parishioners that looking at me was enough to question your belief in God. Momma overheard it, too, so we left that church and found another.

Four more contestants were disqualified, one after another. It was down to me and some brainiac who kept nervously cracking his knuckles.

"Contestant thirteen," came the booming voice.

I stood.

When the judge looked at the computer screen this time, he took his time. He called all the other judges over. They conferred, then sat down again, looking back and forth to one another. When the head judge got on the microphone, he didn't offer me a word to spell. He offered me his apologies.

"I'm sorry, Miss DeFido . . . but the rules are very strict," he said. "We have no choice but to give you the word that comes up on the screen. You understand?"

I nodded.

"There's nothing we can do about it."

I nodded.

He took a deep breath and said, "Please spell . . . *grotesque.*"

And this time there was unrestrained laughter in the audience; the chuckling, twittering voices of students, and parents, too. This was no accident. Somewhere out there, I knew, there was one kid, or two, or a whole gaggle of them who were secretly gloating over having somehow pulled this prank.

I knew what I had to do. Holding my head as high as I could manage, I spelled the word.

"Grotesque," I said. *"G-O . . ."* I leaned closer to the microphone. *"T-O . . ."* I grabbed the microphone stand like a rock star. *"H-E . . ."* I looked out over all those people in the audience. *"L-L.* Grotesque."

Silence from the judges. Silence from the audience.

Finally, the head judge leaned toward his microphone. "Uh . . . I'm sorry," he said. "That is incorrect."

Then, in the front row, a newspaper photographer stood up and brought his camera to his eye.

Go on, take my picture, I thought. *Go on. I dare you.*

And I smiled for him, as wide as I could, stretching my lips over my terrible teeth.